I0639684

praise for HOW WE FRACTURE

"The lives of the women and girls in Karen George's *How We Fracture* are rendered in exquisite detail as they mourn, covet, bear witness, seek the truth and fall in love. These compelling stories are a strong testament to the power of women and girls to navigate a complex world."

— Ellen Birkett Morris, author of
Lost Girls

"*How We Fracture* is an outpouring of sixteen short stories, encircling a startlingly wide sweep of human emotion and experience. At the point of 'fracture', characters encounter loss and fear, doubt and indecision; they also break through into hope and unforeseen new life. Karen George's keen observations—of both the human and the natural world—are revelatory. At the core of this beautiful collection are the complexities and intricacies of love: the setbacks and betrayals as well as the moments of dazzling beauty."

— Eleanor Morse, author of
Margreete's Harbor and *White Dog Fell from the Sky*

"*How We Fracture* is a captivating literary collection that gives readers incredible insight into the lives of women facing pivotal moments of fracture. With sixteen phenomenal stories, George expertly weaves together narratives that span generations, giving voice to characters ranging from teenagers to women in their fifties and sixties. George fearlessly explores a wide range of complex issues in a way that is elegant and evocative. These stories serve as a reminder that despite our individual struggles, we are all connected by the shared experiences and emotions that shape us. George's collection will leave a lasting impression on anyone who reads it. Once again, George has illustrated her masterful ability to take readers on a journey they will never forget."

—Angela Jackson-Brown, author of
The Light Always Breaks

HOW WE FRACTURE

Karen George

MINERVA RISING PRESS
Boca Raton

Copyright © January 2024 Karen George

All rights reserved. No part of this book may be reproduced in any form or by any electronic or mechanical means, including information storage and retrieval systems, without permission in writing from the publisher, except by reviewers who may quote brief passages in a review.

ISBN 978-1-950811-20-5

Printed and bound in USA
First Printing January 2024

Published by Minerva Rising Press
17717 Circle Pond Ct
Boca Raton, FL 33496

Dedicated to the memory of
my mother Vivian, her sister
Marilyn, and my unforgettable
fraternal aunts: Alvera, Theresa,
Dorothy, Rosemary, Marcella,
and Betty.

stories ─────────────────────────

Palindromes

Anna entered my life a mystery, and left the same way. She started mid-semester of my junior year at Dixie Heights High School, 1970. Her family moved to the U.S. from Belgium. She reminded me of Audrey Hepburn, who I'd fallen in love with while watching *Breakfast at Tiffany's*. Anna's pale, unblemished skin looked dramatic against her black pixie haircut, her thick brows, dark eyes accentuated by eyeliner and thick mascara. I wasn't allowed to wear makeup to school even though I complained that my eyes disappeared because of my blonde lashes. She stood out from me and the other students with our long, straight hair; and she dressed like a goth before it became popular—black body-hugging dresses that reminded me of Morticia on *The Addams Family* TV show.

She competed on our school's swim team, winning first place in fly and breaststroke every meet to my reliable second place finish. Her bathing suit was glossy black. I couldn't stop staring at the skeleton tat on her right bicep—a skull with large, exotic flowers blooming from ear, eye, nose, and mouth holes. Toward the semester's end she quit the team due to rotator cuff tendinitis, similar to the bursitis my mother suffered from because of bowling on two different teams year-round.

In Speech Class we were assigned to give a fifteen-minute talk about ourselves, which terrified me. We also needed to prepare it as a paper, between 1,500 and 2,000 words. What would I say about myself for that long?

Anna's speech began with a request that we call her Anna. Her full name was Leigh Anna Lee. She wrote it on the chalkboard in elegant, slanted cursive, the last stroke of each word a rising spiral. Tapping each word with the chalk, she said her name was almost a palindrome, "a word, line, number, or sentence reading the same backward as forward." *Palindrome*, she added to the blackboard. With a graceful turn of wrist, she moved her arm back and forth, waist-level, like an ocean wave advancing and retreating.

The collar of her solid black swing dress was embroidered with white spiderwebs. Patchworked white bats cascaded along her hipline, wings stretched open—an inverse silhouette. When Anna told us she'd sewn the dress, someone snickered. Mom began teaching me to sew a year ago, but I didn't have the confidence to wear my homemade clothes to school.

My first name was Anna, which was a perfect palindrome. If I changed my middle name, Lee, to match the spelling of Anna's first name, Leigh, we'd be palindromes of each other—reverse twins.

Anna revealed her birthdate, 25th of September, 1952 (2591952), (seven days before mine), was a palindrome, same as her four siblings' given names: *Otto, Bob, Hannah,* and *Ada.* She spoke in the level, self-assured tone of a seasoned actress. Mesmerized me with her precise recitation of other palindrome words. *Eye, ewe, eke, gag, pop,* (*poop*, someone behind me whispered), *deed, noon, radar, refer, tenet, reviver.*

In Belgium she'd lived in a city named Ghent that was 607 kilometers, equivalent to 377 miles, from the North Sea where her family visited the Nieuwpoort beaches in summer. Goosebumps rose on my arms, because there was a town in my own state of Kentucky named Ghent, fifty miles away, and one named Newport (pronounced same as Nieuwpoort) four miles away.

She told our class that Ghent, Belgium was known for its medieval monasteries dating back to the seventh century, and castles built in the 1000's. The Ghent Belfry, a tower between St. Bavo's Cathedral and St. Nicholas' Church, held a fiery dragon which guarded the city. She said a canal flowed through the city, linking the Meuse and Scheldt rivers to a lake and other canals.

Anna loved to kayak. "Another palindrome," she said. Her family's backyard butted up against the forest that edged Doe Run Lake. "It's an amazing feeling to paddle for a few strokes, then just glide, like you've slipped inside the water's seam." She closed her eyes, and floated her hand, as though caressing the lake's skin.

Someone whispered, "Give me a break."

I sat in the front row. I could see her dangling earrings—hovering bats—ready to swoop for an insect.

She hoped to one day own a racecar, "Yes, another palindrome." Loved the music of Jimi Hendrix, Jefferson Airplane and The Doors; her favorite songs: "Purple Haze," "Somebody to Love," "White Rabbit," "Break on Through," "People are Strange," "Touch Me." I owned and adored the albums of those same groups.

Students called Anna belittling names, behind her back of course. After her talk, they added *kook* to their list of labels. I wanted to tell her I loved her speech, but never found an opportunity before our junior year ended. Rarely saw her in the halls, cafeteria, or school parking lot—as if she vanished when classes ended. Once she died, her mockers deified her.

I'll never forget the last day I saw Anna at Beechwood Swim Club, the Thursday before Labor Day weekend. I didn't know she belonged; had never seen her there before. I spent almost every day at the pool during summer vacation, either in swim team practice, lifesaving class, or working the concession stand. I wondered if Anna's family had just bought a membership, and if she'd join the swim team.

My stomach fluttered when I approached her on my way to the diving board. All in black—swimsuit, sunglasses, wide brim straw hat, flip-flops— she sat on a dark beach towel in an Adirondack chair. I smiled and waved, but she didn't respond. She might have been asleep. I couldn't tell with her extra-dark lenses. We weren't friends. I'd never spoken more than a few words to her during a school swim meet.

Her shoulders gleamed golden with suntan lotion. A silver lizard bracelet circled her left wrist, and an exquisite new tattoo graced the bicep of the same arm: a black lizard with Jim Morrison's face superimposed over its midsection, *Lizard King* inked in its spiraling tail.

I owned the Doors' *Waiting for the Sun* album that contained the song "Not to Touch the Earth," which ended with Morrison proclaiming, "I am the Lizard King, I can do anything." A chill traveled through me.

I intended to dive off the three-foot springboard but found myself climbing the ladder to the ten-foot, heart rate rising with each step. It wasn't the first time I jumped off the high board, but I'd never dived off it. All summer I tried to overcome my fear of heights. I walked to the end, bounced a few times, returned to the ladder. Arms at my side, head level, I took five measured steps, swung my arms first behind, then above me, as I raised one knee to hurdle into the jump. I rose above the board, tucked chin to chest, folded myself in half to touch my toes, straightened and tightened my body, reached for the water with pointed fingers. What a rush—to break the surface, slice through cold water, push hard off the concrete bottom to burst back into air and sun.

Four days later, on the 7th of September, they pulled Anna's body out of Doe Run Lake. Our senior year began the next day. Apparently, she went kayaking alone, which wasn't unusual. On the local TV news interview, her parents kept repeating that their daughter was an excellent swimmer, a champion kayaker back in Belgium.

You can imagine the rumors at school, students whispering that the 7th of September, 1970 was a palindrome date. That she was born and died on a palindrome date. *So what,* I wanted to scream at them.

I can still see Anna sunbathing that day. When I returned to my beach towel after executing a perfect jackknife, I put on my sunglasses and turned toward her as I dried off, fifteen feet away. From the armrest of her chair, a transistor radio dangled by the strap of its leather case. I couldn't distinguish what song played, but her lizard earrings swayed along with her shoulders, reminding me how she floated her arm in a fluid, dreamy wave during her palindrome presentation.

Toward the end of her speech, she revealed she was the youngest child, and her mother's easiest delivery. She curled her hand closed, raised her arm, let it fall, fingers unfurling like a fern frond. "Mom said I just slid out."

I hope Anna slipped into death the same way. Mouthing words to her favorite song as the water tucked her in.

What We Throw Away

Gabriella owned more than she needed. I decided to make her my summer project, find out what it was like to be rich. I didn't know her real name, so I chose to call her Gabriella. I first saw her and her dog Butch last year, when I ventured onto Devereaux Lane to sell World's Finest Chocolate for my high school. The Land of the Rich nestled beyond the dirt hills behind our house, separated from us by Heaven's Gate Cemetery.

My bike turned out to be the perfect vehicle for snooping. I'd received it last month on my fourteenth birthday. Mom found it at a yard sale.

As I pedaled onto Devereaux Lane, I wondered why these rich people allowed us to live so close to them. There were families on my street that eked by on welfare. The Devereaux Lane people were here first with their English Tudors of subdued colors; no cheap siding or wood painted hot-pink like on my street. On the steep roofs, decorative pots topped each chimney. You know you're rich when you spend money on something smoke pours out of.

For cover, I carried an envelope filled with St. Agnes raffle tickets, prepared to sell them if confronted. The raffle's already over, but they'd never notice. I'd been exploring Devereaux Lane for years, and no one had ever asked who I was or why I was in a neighborhood I didn't belong. Rich people only see what they want to see, what fits within their world.

I rode my bike along a walk made of muted tones of brown and beige bricks, arranged in a herringbone pattern. Between the bricks, blades of glossy grass pushed through. They felt spongy as my tires rolled over them. I stashed my bike beneath a fragrant pine, sticky with sap, the bottom branches sagged almost to the ground. I entered the alley, a continuous brick walkway behind all the houses on each side of the street. One edge butted up against the back of the houses, the other against the woods, separated by a six-foot-high brick wall. Trees overhung the alley, letting through very little light, so I called it a tunnel. A secret passageway, magical and creepy. Any minute I could be discovered and arrested for trespassing, which made it all the more exhilarating. Behind each house, built into the bricks, an open-ended shed held garbage cans, lawn mowers, and weed-whackers. The bricks in the entire tunnel were arranged in decorative patterns, their surface aged and crumbling in some spots.

Devereaux Lane dead-ended into a small private park with a gazebo and knot gardens. The plants were identified by stakes with decorative lettering: marjoram, thyme, sage, chamomile, rosemary, oregano, dill, basil. So many colors and textures to trail my fingers through and smell.

I slung a carryall over my shoulder, filled with my binoculars, raffle tickets, Ziplocs of various sizes, and plastic gloves. At 9:01 a.m. I arrived at Gabriella's house, a cream and dark beige English Tudor. Our entire house would no doubt fit in their guest bathroom. The chimney pots on Gabriella's house had a grid of raised insignias that looked like bound sheaths of wheat. I remembered seeing the same emblem on their front door, maybe their coat of arms.

Last spring, when they opened the door to me and my World's Finest Chocolate, I saw a huge foyer with marbled and inlaid tile of beige and white. A suspended light, larger than our kitchen table, of crystal and leaded glass hung from the ceiling. They bought three candy bars. I doubted they ate them. Probably only indulged in chocolates flown in from Belgium. Maybe they gave them to their maids or butler for Christmas presents. Dad said rich people were the tightest, stingiest people alive. He used to deliver laundry for Chelsea Cleaners, where his boss said the rich never paid their bills until they were two months overdue.

"Sotherfeld" had been etched in bronze on the door knocker. An older woman, probably Gabriella's mother, had answered the door. It surprised me that a butler or maid hadn't come to the door. Maybe it was their day off, or Gabriella's family didn't believe in hired help. Dad said the rich never trusted anyone. That's how they held onto their money.

The woman's cool green eyes looked right past me. She wore all ivory. Lined wool crepe slacks, impeccably creased, silk blouse with mother of pearl buttons. I knew fabrics. Besides my father working for a dry cleaner, my mother altered clothes for Gidding-Jenny's, where she said women paid five hundred dollars for one dress.

From the alley I could see Gabriella's window, located on the side back corner of the house. A narrow casement window with small panes of glass held together with lead in criss-cross patterns. Through my binoculars, I watched her slip into an ivory linen double-breasted blazer. Under the collar and lapels she tucked a filmy scarf, its ends swaying above her slim waist. Thick auburn hair grazed her shoulders with only a suggestion of wave, and shine only money bought. The only way my light blonde turned that shiny was when the public pool contained too much chlorine, which made my hair glisten green.

Gabriella's pantyhose came from France, in a sturdy box painted with pink, lilac, and yellow roses, the nylons nestled between pale blue paisley tissue. In the garbage behind her house, I'd found a discarded box and tissue paper, clean and not crumpled. I used it to store sketches of fashions I designed. Rich people didn't make messes. They owned disposals to put leftover food down, and their maids rinsed off ice cream cartons until no sticky traces remained. You found out a lot about people by digging through their garbage.

Minutes later, Gabriella left in her red Jaguar convertible with a white top. Jags were okay, but if I had Gabriella's money, I'd buy an Austin Healey Roadster, a Ferrari Bentley, or an Alfa-Romeo Spider.

I figured she worked as a guide in The Taft Art Museum, or managed The Netherland Hilton in downtown Cincinnati, or hosted at the Maisonette, where Mom said it cost a hundred dollars for one meal of skimpy portions. Or it might be beneath Gabriella to work. Maybe she volunteered at some high-profile charity foundation, or at the Mercantile Library, where you had to pay to belong.

Rod McKuen occupied the largest portion of our podunk library's poetry section, which ought to be a crime. Not one collection of poetry by Mary Oliver, Maxine Kumin, Carolyn Kizer, Jorie Graham, or Louise Gluck—all Pulitzer Prize winners.

I wondered what kind of books Gabriella read? Last summer I spent a lot of time reading true crime and mass murder books. The concept of a sociopath intrigued me, but I didn't have any desire to hurt anyone.

Two weeks ago, a maid caught me going through a garbage can behind a house at the end of Gabriella's street. I told the maid I'd run away from home and was hungry. I'm not sure she believed me, but she brought me out some muffins. Best I ever tasted, filled with nuts, seeds, and dried fruits. I found a discarded paint wheel while she went inside for muffins. I spent time each day spreading the fan of color chips, picking my favorite shades, recording their dreamy names: Mandalay ivory, sashay sand, veiled violet, cachet cream, abalone shell, Belize blue.

Wearing plastic gloves, I opened one of Gabriella's garbage cans, and found a letter addressed to Judith, Gabriella's real name. I preferred to call her Gabriella, because she looked sweeter than a Judith.

The letter had evidently been hand-delivered. There was no recipient address on the envelope, only a return address. Why would anyone throw away a love letter, even if they weren't interested in the person who wrote it? They might never get another one in their lifetime. Had Gabriella's mother or the maid found it, and threw it out, jealous or over-protective? The letter read:

> *Dear Judith,*
>
> *I know you say it will never work between us. I know it's not fair of me to ask you to live a different life than you're used to. But I can't help asking you. Aren't all your possessions, your status in society worth giving up for the happiness you'd find with me? I love you more than you'll ever be loved. I believe you love me as well. I can promise to love and provide for you to the best of my ability, for as long as I live. Isn't that all anyone can hope for? Please give me a chance to make you happy.*
>
> *Love,*
>
> *Peter*
>
> *P.S. Meet me under the third umbrella at 7:00. I can't wait to hold you in my arms, feel you against me.*

I knew Gabriella had not met Peter. If she had, she would have hidden his letter in a safe place: underneath the lavender velvet lining of her jewelry box, between the pages of her journal slid under the mattress, or the bottom of her underwear drawer pressed between cream lace panties.

Raoul wasn't the man's real name, but I liked the sound of it better. Peter sounded like a nerd's name. I read Raoul's letter to Gabriella over and over. It deserved an answer. I wrote several letters of reply, not intending to mail them. They all ended the same: I would forever cherish his undying love, but could not continue to see him. I wanted to ask Gabriella and Raoul so many questions. How had they met? Was he married? Dying from a rare, incurable disease? Would he give her up easily, or would he stalk her?

Gabriella returned home at 5:10 p.m. She left her car parked in the driveway. Maybe she planned to meet Raoul later.

I hid my bike and moved into position in the tunnel behind her house. My khaki shorts and T-shirt blended in with the tunnel's back brick wall. In the cool and dark passage, I thought of myself as in the underbelly of the rich people's world. Through binoculars I watched Gabriella remove her linen jacket. She dangled it from her hand for a second, examining the wrinkles at the elbows and lower half. Better quality linen than I'd ever seen, its sheen subtle. I could almost feel its grainy texture. Her arm moved as if she tossed the jacket on her bed, or over a chair arm. No doubt dry-cleaned it every time she wore it. Mom wouldn't let us buy clothes unless they were wash and wear—and we didn't wash them after each wear.

I knew that in a few minutes Gabriella would emerge from her front door, to walk her dog down to the park at the end of the street. I hurried along the brick alley, and hid behind a thick trunk, a few feet into the woods at the edge of the park. The bark reminded me of the strong smell of wet wool.

I saw Gabriella's dog first. He stood a foot high and long, gray and white. Tufts of pure white fur flounced at the end of its tail and paws, with a fluffy mane around its face. On the Internet I'd discovered it was a rare breed from France, called a Lowchen. Mom said dogs cost too much to feed, they tear things up, carry diseases, smell up a house. But what if I found a dog, fed it with table scraps I sneaked, made a bed for him in the deserted cabin in the woods down by the railroad overpass off Amsterdam Road? When it got really cold, I'd build a fire in the hearth. I could train it not to bark, even sneak it into my bedroom at night once in a while, let him sleep with me.

I hoped the dog wouldn't smell or sense me. I held my breath as I leaned with my binoculars to see Gabriella, forty feet away. She wore a pearl-colored georgette shirt tucked into silver-gray gabardine slacks and a thin black leather belt. All her clothes fit as if tailored for her body, mostly pastel colors like seafoam, golden wheat, and Rubens beige-pink. It wouldn't hurt her to step out and wear a true-red scarf once in a while. Red's my favorite color.

When I wasn't investigating Gabriella, I spent time in Banasch's Fabrics, going through pattern books, pulling patterns from the drawers, fingering fabric on bolts, planning what I'd sew from each one. I'd sewn since I was eight. Mom started me hemming pants and skirts for Gidding-Jenny's at eight, at nine moved me up to sleeves and shoulders. For my tenth birthday, I received my first Simplicity and McCall's patterns. I preferred Butterick and Vogue, but they cost more.

I used the money from my paper route last year to purchase ivory linen to make a blazer like Gabriella's. I didn't have enough to buy the pale gold lining I wanted, so I pieced remnants of light beige leopard-spotted polyester for the lining. Who cared? No one saw it. Lining's lining, Mom said.

Through my binoculars I studied the fluid way Gabriella's shirt draped, imagining how the fabric would feel against my skin. As I watched the way Gabriella glide-walked as if on a runway, I slid into daydreams of becoming a fashion designer. Hand-sewn lace would be my signature, not the cheap, sleazy Fredericks of Hollywood variety. Mom said a girl can't wear lace until she's sixteen, but I wear lace panties anyway, hand wash them in the bathroom sink, hang them to dry on the register in my bedroom. I have my eye on a pair of ivory lace ones at J.C. Penney's.

Gabriella walked her dog on one of those fancy chains that retract and unwind with the push of a button. I don't believe she cared about him. Never petted him. No wonder he looked unhappy, dressed in a lavender ruffled sweater. Gabriella didn't look happy either. Watching them, I came to the conclusion that her dog was just another one of her accessories, like her tennis bracelet, something to show off her thin wrist.

Whenever the dog tried to step outside of his designated parameters, Gabriella called his name, not bothering to hide her irritation. He was named Jasper, but I renamed him Butch, because he needed a hard-boiled name with his prissy looks.

Ilooked up Raoul's return address on a map in the library. He lived six blocks from me. One afternoon I investigated Prospect Avenue. His house was a large three-story, almost as old as Gabriella's, but run down. I imagined his apartment on the top floor, pictured him in the turret writing long impassioned letters to her. He painted as well, filling canvas after canvas with his beloved's image. In fits of rage he slashed them with a straight razor, and contemplated slitting his wrists with the same edge. Or maybe he worked as a paleontologist, or a poet who wrote love sonnets, exquisite as Neruda's. Gabriella did not deserve Raoul.

Every day I stopped by his apartment, wondering what he looked like. After three weeks I was finally rewarded when Raoul pulled up in a Julio's Plumbing truck. I decided to rename him Raphael instead of Raoul. His pale, angelic skin looked every bit as soft as Gabriella's. He tied his long blonde hair in a ponytail, loose tendrils framing his face. He had a long thin nose, a little hawkish, but I like big noses. My nose is big. Everyone I know who has a big nose wants to get it fixed. Not me. Gabriella had a perfectly formed Anglo-Saxon nose, which most people would kill for.

Raphael wore laced-up leather work boots, snug blue jeans with ratty hems, and an emerald green plaid flannel shirt. He removed a large case from the truck. A cello? I imagined him playing in the tower by the light of the moon, impassioned concertos like Susan Sarandon in *The Witches of Eastwick*, where she held the cello between her legs and flames erupted.

When I saw the care Raphael took lifting the cello case out of his truck, cradling it in his arms rather than trusting the handle, I knew what I had to do. This man deserved a reply to his letter to Gabriella. I felt bad leading him on, but wasn't it better to let him hope for a while at least? My reply letter read:

> *My dearest Peter,*
>
> *I'm a spoiled brat, who doesn't know when she sees a good thing. I've been so sheltered, told what to do for so long. I hope it's not too late to try again. I don't want my parents to find out yet. I need time to see how we work together. I'll contact you as to where and when we can meet. Until then, I'll hold the hope of our love close to my heart.*
>
> *Sweet dreams, my love,*
>
> *Judith*

I typed the letter at the library, dabbed the envelope with Obsession cologne at McAlpin's perfume counter, and pressed Rush Red lipstick to the back of the envelope before mailing it. My lips weren't shaped anything like Gabriella's, but I doubted Raphael would notice. Who knew what condition my lip print would be in when the letter reached his hands? Three days later, when he stepped out of his truck after work, I saw the envelope tucked in his shirt pocket, close to his heart. I felt a little guilty, but who knew, maybe Gabriella would reconsider once he approached her again. But I knew by the scuff of his boots, the length of his hair, the fray of his jeans, that Raphael would never be accepted into Gabriella's family.

On the following Sunday, I watched Raphael drive back and forth down her street, slowing in front of her house. Made me feel sad and guilty. She wasn't home. I'd watched her and her parents back out of their driveway minutes before he arrived. Apparently on their way to church. My family doesn't attend church. Mom said religion's just a way to control people, make them feel like pieces of shit. Who needed that? She might have a point, but I never told her I agreed. Haven't decided what I think of God and church. The way I figure it, God's God, whether I believe or not.

If only Gabriella had delayed one more minute, checking her hair or makeup in her room, she'd have run into Raphael. But I've never seen her check her hair or her makeup. It must be nice to be perfect, but I find perfection boring. I like flaws, try to cultivate as many as I can. Not glaring flaws, but slight imperfections—things just short of the mark. For example, my left eye is higher than my right. You might never notice if I didn't wear glasses. There's a wider gap between the upper rim of my glasses and my eyebrow on the left. Once I discovered it, I cocked my glasses even more, to exaggerate the feature. I liked the disheveled look it gave me, like an absent-minded professor.

Two evenings later, I saw Raphael drive by, hesitate in front of Gabriella's house, circle around and come back the opposite way. He was gone no more than five minutes when Gabriella came out of her house with Butch. I ran down the tunnel to the park, and settled behind a tree. The uneven texture of its trunk reminded me of corduroy with its wale. Gabriella wore ivory linen pants with a champagne-pink tank and cardigan that matched Butch's sweater. He looked humiliated, his pecker hanging out against that color.

As I watched the graceful way Gabriella rose from the stone bench, I wondered who my real parents were. I believed they adopted me. I didn't look like either of them, or my younger sister. I might be the sister of Winona Ryder, George Clooney, Michelle Pfeiffer, Brad Pitt. Or Gabriella. Her mother might have had an illicit affair, gone on an extended stay in the country, given me up for adoption.

My dad left last year. He moved out west to work on a dude ranch, or so Mom said. I imagined him on a horse at the edge of a huge canyon, watching the sunset. I pictured a rattler spooking his horse, plunging them into the canyon, the horse's legs flailing frantically, my father trying to hold on as if he were astride a bucking bronco.

"Jasper, I'm not in any hurry." Gabriella pulled Butch back, forced him to conform to her pace.

When she headed back toward her house, I returned behind the houses through the tunnel, retrieved my bike, and entered the woods for a shortcut home. Thirty feet in, I heard a crashing, crunching sound behind me. I whirled, expecting a troop of skeletons headed toward me. But it was Butch. He bounded into my arms, and before I knew whether he was going to bite me, he licked my face.

Gabriella didn't call for him. Surely she saw the direction he headed. Why didn't she follow? I waited a good ten minutes, telling the dog to shoo, go home. Butch ran back and forth in front of me, charging at my feet, play-snapping at my toes, snarling and yap-yapping to his heart's content. He wasn't dragging his leash. Had Gabriella let him loose on purpose? Maybe she'd grown tired of owning a dog. If you could have anything you wanted, anytime you wanted, maybe things lost their meaning quicker than if you scrimped and saved until you could afford them.

Butch followed me to the deserted cabin by the train tracks. I filled the emerald green bowl I'd brought last week with water from jugs I'd accumulated for months. The way he tore into the beef jerky, I wondered if he'd eaten in a week. I didn't need to show Butch his bed. After a short exploration of the cabin, he went straight for the box piled high with pillows, and a fluffy blanket I found down in the basement at the very bottom of a pile of dirty laundry. Mom never got down that far in the pile.

I didn't return to Gabriella's street for weeks. I wondered if she missed Butch. He didn't miss her. We took long walks in the woods. He chased squirrels, birds, lizards. Free for once in his life, he dug in the dirt and rummaged through weeds. Every night before I went home, I'd pull out the burrs, check for ticks, clean his paws, brush his coat, and stroke his soft waves. I didn't believe Gabriella took nearly as good of care of Butch as I did. Maybe she wanted to, but didn't know how.

He dog-paddled in the lake behind the cabin. I didn't always keep him on a chain. He could have escaped, found his way back to Gabriella. The lost-and-found section of the newspaper never listed any dog missing that fit Butch's description. I worried Mom might eventually notice the food I stole, or the missing money, but I was careful to only take a single or two. As long as I finished my alterations, she never commented on why I was gone from home more than ever.

One night as I emerged from the woods into Heaven's Gate Cemetery, I spotted Gabriella's Jaguar parked at the end of Marlboro Place, near the street light. It freaked me out to see her on my street. For a second I thought she knew I'd stolen her dog, and came to confront my mom. But she wouldn't know where I lived. Then I wondered if she was making out with Raphael, but I only saw her silhouette.

Had she followed me? Hiding behind a rusted-out pickup, I leaned to see inside her car through my binoculars. I had a front view. The light through the windshield illuminated her like a spotlight onstage. Palms covered her face, her shoulders convulsed. I couldn't believe it. What in the world could Gabriella have to be so upset about? She had more money than she knew what to do with, and a man crazy in love with her. Hell, plenty of men probably wanted her. And here she sat, crying, in my neighborhood.

I watched her a while longer, amazed by the intensity of her emotion, again wondering what could cause her such grief. Finally I lowered my binoculars and walked home. It no longer felt right spying on such a private moment. Was she that upset about her dog's disappearance? Had she finally given up hope of finding him? Had someone she loved died? Was she pregnant by a man who wanted nothing to do with her and his child? I couldn't imagine her parents happy about that news. Mom always said whatever I do, don't get pregnant, and expect her to raise any of my bastards.

For the next couple days, I couldn't get the picture of Gabriella crying out of my mind. Alone in her car, in my trashy neighborhood. What did she have to hide, and what couldn't she share with her family? I knew what that felt like. My family didn't know anything about who I really was. Maybe Gabriella's family didn't understand her either. I wanted to be happy about that, to feel revenge or something I didn't even have a name for, but it saddened and scared me to think that even rich people had problems.

I never intended to keep Butch forever. What's a month in a dog's lifetime? I couldn't keep him once I went back to school. He wouldn't last in that unheated cabin in the winter, and I wouldn't have time to mess with him once I found an after-school job. If I earned my own money, I could get an apartment in a year or two, start my own life. I couldn't help but wonder why Gabriella still lived with her parents. Surely she had enough money to live on her own. She had to be in her late twenties. What kept her living at home?

I thought of carrying Butch to Gabriella's house, saying I found him wandering in the woods. Might get reward money. Instead I wrote a letter, telling her how happy I was with Jasper, and how lucky she was (in case she didn't realize it) to have a beautiful dog, and live in a huge house, and own classy clothes, and a hot sports car. I wrote that I hoped she and Peter lived a happy life together. But in the end I tore the letter in tiny pieces and threw them off the Roebling Suspension Bridge into the Ohio River. What did a fourteen-year-old know about a rich woman's life?

Whenever I wear my linen blazer with the leopard lining, I think of Judith. Mine wasn't as good quality as hers, but it was washable linen. I wondered how things worked out with Peter? At this exact moment, he might be pressing against Judith's linen, fingering her silken hair.

Never again have I spied on Judith or anyone else on Devereaux Lane. Instead I decided to concentrate on reading about the top female fashion designers. They were complicated enough for now.

A brilliant idea occurred to me, a true gift to Judith, whether she deserved it or not. I spent one last day with Jasper. We visited the lake, chased squirrels and ducks, tore through the cemetery where he pissed on more than one gravestone. I rode him in my bicycle basket to Riverside Drive, walked him along the Ohio, across the suspension bridge. For our last supper, we ate Skyline chili-dogs on the bench alongside the bronze statue of James Bradley reading.

I imagined Jasper happy with Judith. In his dreams, he remembers the blond girl who used to let him ride in her bicycle basket, and how the wind ruffled and tickled his fur. How he ran through the deep woods with all its scents until he thought he'd explode with happiness.

In the middle of the night, I climbed out of my bedroom window, took Jasper from the cabin, wrestled him into the coat I'd crocheted, and tied him to the passenger door of Peter's truck. He'd see Jasper when he came out of his apartment in a couple of hours. I asked Jasper not to bark, gave him two big pig's ears and a bowl of crispy bacon. He was sad to see me go, though he never looked up. Who could blame him? He was knee deep in pork products.

Tickling under his chin one more time, I memorized the fringe of his ears, the velvet wave of his fur, his earthy musk.

The Floating Child

I wanted to tell Mother my secret in a wide open space, among trees and birds, where we had something to look at, besides each other. I hoped to prepare her for the shock. Father had been admitted to St. Vivian's Hospital hours earlier. His emphysema had worsened to the point where inhalers and nebulizers proved ineffective. When the gurney arrived to transport him downstairs for a series of tests, his nurse suggested we leave for lunch. I drove to Muller's Deli, weighing the words to tell my mother I was pregnant and wanted to abort the baby.

The possibility of carrying a child and giving birth created an avalanche of wonder and expectation within me, but I'd planned for so long to attend art school, study The Masters, visit all the great museums. Since learning of my pregnancy, some days narrowed to the pinpoint center of a spiral. Others expanded outward. I drew detailed minutia, then large swathes of color: ants, bees, dragonflies, eyes, ears, and wrinkles on knuckles, to bridges, cathedrals, rivers, mountains, and canyons.

Mother had chosen River Bend Park for its old trees and river view, things we both loved. We ate havarti cheese and sweet red pepper sandwiches, seated in the garden, side by side on a wrought-iron loveseat, overlooking the Kentucky River where it snaked east toward Pine Mountain. I wondered if she, like me, tried not to worry about Father. Sixty-three, he'd smoked since the age of twelve, worked in a tobacco factory all his life. He continued smoking, despite his emphysema, but only on the back deck since Mother's diagnosis of breast cancer last fall.

The open air diluted the smell of her skin, but every so often I caught a whiff that reminded me of a cast-iron skillet. That heavy smell grated against the sweet scent of the red peppers on my sandwich. I studied the thick live oak branches tilting toward earth, trying not to see Mother's wrists, so thin and pale yellow.

I still couldn't believe a baby floated inside me. When I was young, I pictured myself with children. Born late in my parents' life, an only child, I suspected they neither planned nor wanted me. I swore my life would be different. Now this pregnancy, at the worst possible time, disease and death lurking in our house. Those very threats paired me with Ryan. I longed to touch and be touched.

Mother took a deep breath. "It's hard to feel bad when it's spring."

I followed her eyes from the fallen flowers of the star magnolia to the pale pink dogwood blossoms open like hands to receive. She seemed to relax as she looked at the trees, as if this was just what she needed, to immerse herself in spring's growth. I tried not to imagine what she'd say when I told her. Would she remind me that our family descended from a line of staunch Catholics? I imagined her asking me why I couldn't carry her to term, (I was convinced it was a girl), and give her up for adoption. But one of the girls in my homeroom class gave her child away. She hung herself a year later.

I prayed for the right words as I calmed myself, noticing how Mother also stared at the cornucopia before us. Swathes of orange, yellow, and cream daffodils swayed beneath silver maples with leaves cocooned in tight buds, waiting to uncurl. Mr. Wessler, the master gardener at the nursery where I worked weekends, told me trees and flowers contained blueprints, beginning with the seeds, detailing every increment of their life cycles. This innate knowledge directed their response to changes in temperature and light, so they knew when to rise through soil, when to open blossoms, when to disperse seeds. I wondered what inklings curled within human embryos.

Mother glanced around. "Do you mind if I take my hat off?"

I tried not to envision her bare head, how much it exposed, so quickly, wondering what if I said no. But she didn't wait for my answer before she removed the straw hat and anchored its wide brim beneath her purse. Perhaps she suspected what I'd say. I didn't want to see her bare head. During the first round of chemo treatments, her hair fell out in patches, revealing a scalp the color of raw salmon. She rarely took the hat off, even at home. It was so odd to see her remove it here, as if she were ready to uncover something important, as if she knew both of us were waiting for something to happen.

Looking straight ahead, I imagined the russet waves of her hair shining in the sun, even though my peripheral vision revealed a skull unprotected as a newborn's. Did she have any hint of what I hid? I waited to hear her ask why Ryan hadn't been around. She had to wonder why I wouldn't accept his calls. I'd graduate in two weeks, and then I'd be less likely to encounter him, but how long would it take for me to not miss his touch?

Mother talked about how Father tried to hide from her his inability to breathe. He looked so frail, as if the light could show right through his skin. She hoped he didn't have to stay in the hospital, but she didn't mention any hopes about his tests. Mother rarely talked to me about how she felt. I didn't know how to respond. It took me by surprise that she'd overstepped the boundaries of our world. No maps existed from that point on. An unspoken code, part of our DNA, ingrained from our German heritage, demanded we restrain our emotions, and imply affection rather than display or declare it. But, I'd trampled all the boundaries with my unwanted pregnancy. It felt as if I floated in the river's current, unanchored, nothing to ground me.

As I sat beside Mother, clutching the remaining triangle of my sandwich, I thought about what I could say to lead into my revelation, but I couldn't bring myself to speak. Instead I said, look at the redbud.

I couldn't stop myself from imagining a daughter to unfold the beauty of nature for, and share in the excitement of her discoveries. I'd tell her about the Newport plum to our left with pink lace blossoms smelling of almonds, the Bradford pear flaunting white confetti, and the ash with its crusty strips of bark waving in the wind.

Behind us sassafras trees swished shadows left to right, releasing a root beer scent. My body wanted to follow their luxurious rhythm. I looked down to restrain myself, to remind myself of what I needed to do. I could no longer bear to wonder. Or imagine how it might be different if my parents were healthy, if I were older, married. How to carry and nurture a child might open up my art, my life.

I took a deep breath, bringing myself back, seeing my scuffed white gym shoes against the red bricks, hearing Mother's nylon jacket swish against my denim shirt sleeve as she raised the sandwich to her mouth. The sun cast the loveseat's tiny interlocking diamond grid with the shadows of our seated frames onto bricks spiraling to a center bronze sundial. The shadows of our bodies leaned toward each other, almost touching.

I didn't expect the park with all spring's abundance to affect me so intensely. My fingers ached to hold my sketch book, to translate this intricate network of light and dark. I wanted to immerse myself in all the blossoms, tranquilize myself. But it also heightened my awareness. The undeniable fact. My body cradled its own evolution, cells dividing and multiplying even as I tried to fathom words to say, to divine Mother's reaction.

Studying the shadows near my shoes, I remembered Mr. Wessler explaining how sassafras trees grew three leaf shapes: unlobed, two-lobed like a mitten, and three-lobed, often on the same branch. I knew nothing of a fetus' formation, but I imagined my baby floating and unfolding within me. As I swallowed, I thought about how the organs of my body connected to transform cheese, bread, and peppers into vitamins and minerals, nourishing all the way down to the cellular level. When we're done eating, I told myself, I'll tell her then. I tried not to fidget.

If only I could have shared my secret with my friends Laura and Janet. I had planned to, until last week, when members of the local "Right to Life" organization visited our school. After their presentation, Janet asked how anyone could kill a baby, and Laura shook her head in disbelief. I shrugged when they turned to me. Said I didn't know what I felt about abortion. Maybe it was an abomination. But even as I lied to them, in my heart I knew it wasn't right to judge anyone who decided to abort a baby, especially when the condemners never faced an unwanted pregnancy.

There I sat, nearly holding my breath. After swallowing every last smidgen of my sandwich, I closed my hands into fists, pressing nails into the soft pads of my palms. I stretched my legs out in front of me. Mother's legs were bent back beneath the bench, as if she was trying to curl up for warmth. She threw pieces of crust toward the ash tree. The motion vibrated the metal beneath us. Her other hand lay in her lap, tightened around the breadcrumbs. Fat-bodied doves waddled to reach them, tiny heads bobbing. I don't know why, but she started talking about the farm her grandparents owned, the land sold before I was born. Smiling toward the river, no doubt seeing that land spread before her, she asked me to close my eyes and listen. She mimicked bird calls: red-winged blackbird, finch, cardinal. Her rendition of the dove's mournful sound saddened yet soothed me. She said Grandma claimed bird songs held the secret of life, if you decoded them. How I longed to tell Mother my secret, but without hurting her. She'd been through so much with her cancer and Dad's emphysema. How could I bring more pain into her life, into mine?

We didn't talk for a while, eyes closed, listening side by side, breathing slowed and synchronized. The odd thing was, in that silence, I'd never felt so close to my mother. Could she sense my confusion, my inability to speak? Maybe I exuded signals only the woman who birthed me could interpret. It felt as if my body hummed, intent as a bee's buzz. I couldn't stop myself from returning to the scenarios I'd fantasized about, where in the midst of all the spring growth, I revealed she was going to be a grandmother. What joy there'd be, and an added incentive for her to fight the cancer, to live. Maybe I could whisper my secret in her ear.

But there she sat, watching the chickadees hide seeds in the branches, palms cupped open in her lap, as if enticing the birds to land. How could I burden her with my shame, when she had so much to carry already?

I studied her face. Lush, arched eyebrows I used to envy—gone, along with her eyelashes and every trace of hair. It might sound funny, but I missed the tiny, colorless hairs on her face, which you couldn't see unless the sun hit them with just the right light. Her skin, once radiant, now looked thin and too fragile. I had to look away, at the hedge of blazing forsythia. At the grass gleaming liquid green, as only the first spring growth can. Rain the previous night had heightened the scents of sweet soil, and seduced earthworms closer to the surface. I heard her take a deep breath.

"Did you have a fight with Ryan?" She touched my wrist, her skin hot.

"I'm pregnant."

I couldn't believe I'd said those words, just like that, like I'd said I was going shopping or might like to get some ice-cream later. Mother released a drawn out "oh." Heat rose in my eyes, tears pooling. A sensation of rushing forward filled me, a feeling of falling from a great height. No way to take back the words, to stop the growth inside me. No way, but one.

I waited for her to barrage me with questions and accusations. How could I have let this happen? What was I going to do now? How could I be so selfish? Did I realize this would kill Father?

But she didn't speak. Instead she leaned forward, hands braced on her knees. I watched her, thinking at any moment she'd get up, turn, and leave me alone on the loveseat. The nausea of morning sickness rose in me. I took a deep breath, and kept my face toward the river. Patches of purple and white redbuds interspersed with the browns and grays of the woods along the river banks. Clouds overhead left part of the forest in sun, part in shadow. Birds squawked and flapped wings behind us.

"Are you sure?" Her voice cracked.

I hadn't seen Mother cry since our next door neighbor's daughter died from bee stings.

I remember being horrified at the thought of all those bees, but I was more terrified by the way Mother broke down that day of the bees, the way she kept apologizing to us afterward.

I was sure, I said, my voice high and tight.

When her tears came, she dropped her head toward her chest. I thought she'd passed out until she began sliding her palm over her bare scalp as if to wipe it all away. Swallowing hard, I concentrated on the shadow of her arm shifting on the bricks before us; lighter and fuzzier when her hand reached the back of her head, darker and more delineated when she neared her forehead.

She sat up, head tall, and snugged on her hat. "We better get back to the hospital."

I sat there, feeling my breath leave me. I wanted to kick something hard, like a car door. Crunch a huge dent with the heel of my shoe. I wanted to screech, "Did you hear what I said? What are we going to do?"

But we walked to the car silently. I said nothing as Mother took the driver's seat. Bone-tired, I leaned against the headrest, suffocating from the sun beating through the glass combined with the metallic, antiseptic smell emanating from her skin. I sat still as she drove with her eyes fixed straight ahead. She slid into a parking space like water upon a shore. We opened our car doors, but neither of us moved. I couldn't. Not even when she reached over and touched my hand. We'd go to an out-of-town clinic, she said.

I sat very still, her hand light in mine. My mother was telling me to have an abortion. The same decision I'd made. Why didn't I feel relief? There was neither blame nor incomprehension in her tone or words or face. Her voice, soft and steady, gave nothing away. But her eyes avoided mine.

Together we headed toward the visitors' entrance. I tried to shove down the floating question of what my choice would have been if my parents were healthy. Without a word I walked at her side as the three of us passed beneath an arbor supporting a web of Chinese wisteria, their vines in full bloom, their gnarled trunks thick as wrists, their shadows swaddled in fragrance.

Wide-open

Friday morning, before I left for my shift at the hospital, the bank foreclosed on the Farrell's house across the street. I pulled a couple of weeds near my magenta Stargazer lilies to see the sign a man hammered into their front lawn. No one lived there long. The house was cursed. A widower slit his wrists, a woman burned to death, and a man was shot in his bed. Though the Farrells lived there for two years, I didn't know their first names until I asked my neighbor.

After work I watched the Farrell's teenage daughter, Jen, from my front porch. She sat on the steps, brushing her long black hair, eyes closed, sketchbook in her lap, before setting the brush aside. Jen wore her usual —all black clothes and shoes. I wondered what she thought about, where she transported herself to, and who accompanied her. After completing each row of cross-stitches, I allowed myself to hone in on her. I tried not to stare too long. She drew until dark, picking at the supper plate beside her. I remembered the magic of sketching.

I woke around two a.m., same as most nights, and couldn't get back to sleep. From my window seat in the dark, I watched the street, listened to the sugar maple swish in the wind and faint echoes from the railroad tracks. Jack Farrell, the husband, waited up for his wife on their front porch. Everything he wore was some variant of beige. Maybe they'd started out more vibrant in color and had merely faded. On many nights Jack played the harmonica. Haunting melodies that wormed inside you if you weren't careful. Sections of songs he played sounded familiar—dreamy, heartbreaking strains of "Blueberry Hill," "What a Wonderful World," and "Unchained Melody." Mostly I thought he made up his tunes, series of notes that rose and fell, taking me places I didn't want to go. Made me wonder what it would have been like to be my fiancé Samuel's wife, have children, and continue my artwork. But I couldn't stop listening. I thought of sketching Jack in charcoal or painting him. When he reached the end of his current song, he removed his ball cap and raised it in my direction as if to acknowledge applause.

The wife, Alice, worked the late shift at Frisch's restaurant. Her red car pulled up, and she got out with two carry-out bags. They ate on the steps side-by-side under the porch light. The smell of their greasy food fouled the cinnamon spice of my purple petunias in the window box. Alice reminded me of a female wrestler. She rushed at everything. I never saw her straight black hair worn any way but pulled back in a short spiky ponytail, her jaw permanently clenched. How much sadness, how many humiliations did it take to give her such a look?

Jack and Alice were barely inside the house, when they started shouting. They had a major fight every month. Which was their business. I was engaged once, but never married. I suspected marriage was a tightrope walk. How could you determine if the screams had escalated to the point where help was needed? They had enough problems without adding legal complications. By the time police officers arrived, the spur of the fight had worn down. They'd issue another warning that the fights needed to stop. Surely they didn't like fighting? All it added up to was cursing and viciousness.

Growing up, I witnessed enough fights between my parents to last me several lifetimes.

I'd delve into music, bury myself in an art book, anything to block out the yelling. My father struggled with depression. He missed work, which led to lost jobs and escalating debt. Mother worked to stave off bankruptcy. I thought if I got all A's in school instead of that one B in history, if I'd won first place instead of second in Kentucky's high school art contest, if I stayed quiet in my room, maybe I could have saved him. Never could make Samuel understand why I wouldn't argue for what I believed in. He said we needed to break through our differences. I was tired of broken things. Mom threw glasses, plates, jars of mustard and mayonnaise. She never broke through anything, but into deeper rage.

I wondered what the Farrells' daughter thought of all the turmoil. Was she afraid? Embarrassed? Angry? I pictured Jen propped against her headboard, drawing as fast as her fingers could move. Or brushing her hair slowly, carefully, eyes closed, taking slow, deep breaths, imagining a lover to carry her away to Antarctica. A paleontologist. She'd sketch him and new sea species exposed by melting ice.

One time Jen came onto my porch to sell candy for school. She'd asked what I was doing, said she noticed me holding some kind of frame. I explained cross-stitching, and showed her my current project—an old country garden. Before she left, I mentioned that I knew she drew, and would love to see some of her work. She blushed and lowered her head. Not quick enough to hide her grin. I'd almost told her I used to draw.

The Farrells didn't fit in with our neighborhood. We're nowhere near rich and not particularly conceited, but people on our street took pride in their homes, kept up with the house and yard, decorated for the seasons but removed the decorations within a reasonable amount of time after the holiday passed. But no one gave the Farrells a chance, saying they were the kind of hillbillies that gave Kentucky a bad name. People called the police on the husband for his harmonica playing, or when their fights escalated. I reported them once because of their dog, Attila. He barked early mornings, when I slept best, and he tore through my gardens. His back reached almost to my waist. Shiny black coat, eyes so dark they disappeared in his face. When I worked on my gardens near the street, his growl vibrated through me. He knew I was afraid of him.

Someone poisoned Attila last week. Alice discovered his body. A piercing screech woke me at seven a.m. From my front door window I saw her cradle him in her arms, a dog that weighed easily seventy pounds. In the middle of the street she screamed, "I'll kill the bastard that did this!"

While I weeded the back garden, Mrs. Swope motioned me over to the fence separating our yards. Through thin wisps of silver hair, her scalp looked pink like skin after a scab falls off. She wore a blue and white gingham check housedress beneath a white cardigan sweater with mother-of-pearl buttons shaped like rosebuds. Despite my feelings for her, Mrs. Swope's clothes, so dated and innocent, made me want to enfold her in my arms.

"Anna, what do you think about the Farrells?" she asked.

I refused to play along, pretending ignorance, as I had a week earlier when she commented on the "striped kid" up the street. Referring to the biracial family, she wanted to pull me into her bigotry.

"I see they're moving," I said.

"Moving? They got thrown out on their asses."

It wouldn't have surprised me if the venom in her voice shriveled my scarlet peonies a foot away. She'd been a widow for as long as I'd lived in the neighborhood. Evidently childless as well. I should have felt sorry for Mrs. Swope. Maybe I feared turning into her.

"They must have gotten behind on their payments," I said. "It's easy to do these days. Jack must have lost his job."

"I doubt he ever had one. Anyway, I say good riddance. The trash is finally getting taken out to the curb."

I bent to pick up my hand trough, to remind Mrs. Swope that she'd interrupted my work.

She was no doubt lonely. Her bare feet looked swollen in her scuffs. Varicose veins bulged on her calves like earthworms. I looked into her aged face, trying to generate compassion for her. "How're your counts doing, Mrs. Swope?"

She had diabetes. "Not good," she whispered, lowering her head. She began outlining her health issues. The wristbands of her sweater had worked up her arms, revealing large bruises. She mentioned the doctors had a fit keeping her blood thinner medicine at the correct level.

I said I was really sorry to hear that she wasn't feeling well and hoped she'd begin improving. She almost smiled.

Early Saturday, I cross-stitched on the front porch. The light's better outside, especially early morning sun. I was working on a Christmas snow scene for one of the nurses I share a shift with in I.C.U. at St. Elizabeth's Medical Center. Pulling the blue-green thread through the crisp white linen, I formed the branch of a spruce.

My house was built on a slope, so I had a bird's-eye view of the neighborhood. I tried not to stare, only watching for a minute or two in between rows. The Farrells carried out box after box, none taped shut or labeled. Maybe they were moving somewhere closeby. Open boxes with protruding lampshades, blackened fireplace tongs, purple feather duster plumes. Alice and Jen shoved them into their Buick LeSabre. Gouges and dents disfigured the entire driver's side and the back bumper dangled close to the ground. Instead of spreading a tarp over the rusted truck bed and arranging boxes neatly, Jack dropped them with a heavy thud. Some boxes tumbled on their sides, spilling unwrapped rolls of toilet paper, a toilet brush, and plunger. Items remained where they fell, boxes piled on top of them. I didn't understand why they took so little care with their belongings.

Jack burned rubber as he pulled away on one of his trips, the tailgate down. Uncooked pasta, dried potato buds, and grains of rice cascaded onto the street. I wanted to ask if they needed help, but it was too late to act interested in what happened to them.

Few things are as sad as packing. The last time I'd packed, five years ago, was to move from an apartment to this house my fiancé and I bought. I had begun in such bliss, packing up our possessions. Samuel had left to get more boxes from the grocery. He'd never returned, his car found two blocks away near a railroad crossing, engine running, headed in the direction of our apartment.

After a half hour, I figured Kroger's, only five minutes away, had been out of boxes, so he'd gone to the more distant Remke's. Or he stopped at Emerson's Bakery for the lemon squares we loved. He often brought me something sweet after we'd fought. I opened one of my new cookbooks to search for a lemon square recipe, but found only lemon tart, lemon sherbet, lemon poppy seed bread. I made a note to find a lemon square recipe and make them for him the following Saturday while he was at work.

I paged through some of my other cookbooks, dreaming about the meals we'd assemble and share. Samuel loved to cook, was much better at it than me. His mother taught her sons and daughters early on. My mother only passed on her lack of enthusiasm for cooking. But that would change, I told myself, as I looked at the glossy photo of Pecan-Crusted Chicken. I continued to pack thinking about the meals we'd share, feeling more and more full. But the question of what was taking Samuel so long gnawed at me. I called his cell phone. No answer. Battery might be dead. He was lax about keeping it charged. I paged through "The Joy of Cooking," marked some pages with orange, green, and violet tabs, conceiving a series of drawings of a couple sharing meals. I tried not to let my imagination take a dark turn, but I couldn't stop it. Samuel trapped in his blue Mustang, unconscious while Jaws of Life worked to free him. Preoccupied with the fight we'd had, he hadn't seen the semi jackknife toward him. An aneurism in his brain burst. As always, I ended up remembering how I found my father in the garage with the car engine running. I never forgot the fact that if I hadn't stayed at school to find out about the art club before walking home, I might have saved him.

After an hour and a half, I drove to hunt for Samuel. Maybe he ran out of gas and had to walk to a station. I found his Mustang still running. His cell phone lay open on the passenger seat, the screen pattern of turquoise, magenta, and orange spiraling. Had he opened it, preparing to call, and changed his mind? Nothing else remained in the car but eight empty boxes, stacked inside each other, in the back seat. I turned off his engine and waited in his car. Holding my cell phone in one hand, his in the other.

The police investigated, but finding nothing, concluded Samuel left of his own will. His family held me responsible for his disappearance, though they never stated their suspicions to my face. His mother kept asking if we'd had a spat. I wouldn't admit anything, because it was none of her business. We had a disagreement, not a fight, the night before he disappeared, about what I thought we'd already settled. Samuel wanted children. I didn't. He ended up screaming, "What are you afraid of?" Brought up again that he knew something happened to me, to shut me down, and begged me to talk about it. My reply was always the same—some pains are better buried. I wondered if Samuel only agreed to marry me in hopes of cracking my secrets.

I didn't even want to remember how embarrassed I felt telling family, friends, and co-workers of his disappearance. The corners of their eye-lids concealed questions, doubts, and insinuations. Living under every-one's scrutiny terrified me. I'm a private person. Maybe that's why Samuel abandoned me. He said I expressed my feelings exquisitely in my art but remained unable to release them into my life.

For months, like a buzzard, I picked over Samuel's every word and ges-ture before he left the apartment that day, wondering if I said or didn't say something that might have made a difference. I'd moved into the house we bought to share our lives in, the house I still occupy. Unpacked only what I'd needed to exist, hoping to do the remainder when he returned. Trying to keep my hopes alive, I'd delayed the unpacking and separating of my possessions from Samuel's.

I couldn't stop thinking about all the unpacking that awaited the Farrells, and how depressing it would be. I decided to bake two lemon meringue pies. One for them, one for me. While the pies baked, I cross-stitched on the front porch. Bringing the needle up and down in tiny x's through the white linen relaxed me and filled my time. Cross-stitching had quieted my mind and body when I wanted to smash our wedding gifts and shred my bridal gown. I hadn't let myself draw, my rage so intense I feared what I'd create. I'd cross-stitched my way back to feeling half-human.

The parade of the Farrells' possessions continued: a stained mattress, heaps of bed linens and towels and clothes on wire hangers thrown loose into the truck bed. The daughter helped carry a few boxes, but mostly stayed inside. I pictured her stroking page after page, forming the jawbone and deep-set eyes of a Spanish lover, the stone foundation of the castle in which they'd live.

The Farrells didn't speak as they loaded their belongings. I wondered where they were going. Couldn't imagine it being somewhere nicer. I tried not to see their leaden faces. They echoed the numbness I felt when I moved into the house without Samuel. With each tiny cross-stitch I com-pleted, as if marking off rosary beads, I prayed that the Farrell's lives im-proved in their new home.

At dusk, the Farrells pulled away in the Buick. They left the front door open. I crossed the street to close it for them. What I saw through the open door drew me in. Hunks of drywall missing from the living room walls as if bashed with a sledgehammer. The ceiling had collapsed in one corner of the dining room, wires and ducts exposed. Two wall cabinets on the kitchen floor, gouges in the plaster where they had hung. The stovetop, covered with two rusted pots and a crusty skillet, butted up against a wall black and blistered from a fire. I wandered room to room, unable to believe what I saw. Had they lived in these conditions for a while, or had they deliberately done this damage when they learned of the bank's foreclosure? In the backyard an above-the-ground swimming pool, sides caved in, held the skeleton of a once-live Christmas tree with lights, ornaments, and tinsel attached.

I found the Farrell's wedding album balanced on top of an overflowing trash drum. How could they throw away the photos documenting the beginning of their lives together? The first page had an engagement picture. Alice wore a pink dress with a white orchid pinned to a lace collar. Her hair lay in loose, lustrous waves, soft against her clear skin. Jack wore a navy pinstripe suit and a thin solid red tie. Her head rested on his shoulder, as if to say she knew he would always support her. Their faces contained such hope and joy. I closed the album, and breathed deeply to prevent the panic rising in me.

A stack of rumpled sketches lay beneath the album. Intricate mythological creatures, half human, half animal, in decadent costumes. The backgrounds detailed lush fantasies of landscape and architecture. The stack also contained disembodied portraits—faces of a young bald man, with blank backgrounds, rendering intense states of anticipation, joy, disbelief, anger and grief.

Leaving the front door open as I found it, I left with Jen's sketches. Placed them between pages of my book of Impressionistic paintings, saying a prayer that she continued to draw.

When the Farrells returned, I crossed the street to Alice and Jen. Jack had plopped in his chair on the porch. Jen's face was so pale, as if she'd applied white face powder. She wore black nail polish and dark lipstick. A large gold Byzantine cross hung on a long chain above her waist. Alice's chapped face showed a wildness that chilled me. Her black hair streaked with one half-inch white stripe reminded me of a skunk. Her purple T-shirt, cut in a deep vee, revealed more than I cared to see.

"I wanted to wish you happiness in your new home." I extended the pie to Alice. "Lemon meringue."

She accepted the pie, but stared at me with such contempt. I felt sure she was going to hit me.

"Hey, Jack," she yelled in my face. "Lookee what your friend, Little Miss Peeping Anna did. She brought us a pie."

Jack didn't respond. Alice balanced the pie high in the palm of her hand, and flung it against the pavement.

Never had anyone directed such pure hatred toward me. I couldn't turn away from her face, envious of the way she held nothing back. Jen looked at her mother in disbelief, then down at the splattered pie, saying, "What a fucking mess." What freedom, I thought, to say exactly what you felt. The three of us stared at the yellow and cream dots clinging to our calves. I smeared a dollop of lemon cream from my leg onto my finger, licked it off. "You don't know what you're missing," I said.

Inside, I ate two slices of pie, while I read about the total lunar eclipse predicted to happen that night. I couldn't stop thinking about the Farrells. I needed to do something. Reaching my bank just before it closed, I got an anonymous money order for three thousand dollars made out to Jen Farrell. At Border's, I bought three books: drawings of Leonardo da Vinci, William Blake, and a book featuring work by women including Frida Kahlo, Georgia O'Keeffe, Joan Mitchell, Diana Arbus, and Dorothea Lange. When I returned home, Alice and Jen reclined in lounge chairs in Jack's truck bed, faces turned upward, awaiting the lunar eclipse. How great to have a daughter.

I came out on the front porch as the eclipse began. In my chaise lounge, with the light of the streetlamp, I had a perfect view of Alice, Jen, and the diminishing moon. The intense reds filled me with longing. From a bowl in Alice's lap, Jen grabbed handfuls of popcorn. The fresh-popped aroma fused with scents of my alyssum, moonflower, and newly mown grass. The clear night sky swelled with stars, as we witnessed the earth's shadow obscure the moon. Alice and Jen sat with a blanket over their shoulders, reminding me of the time Samuel and I nestled under a sheet tent in the dark. I held a flashlight while he read Gibran's "The Prophet." Between sections, he kissed me.

After the eclipse, I returned inside and cut the tape on the only remaining box of Samuel's possessions, pulling out each item. At the very bottom I found my chalks, charcoals and tubes of paint. My hands trembled as I set them on top of my hope chest. Wrapped in his burgundy cashmere cardigan, surrounded by his wool argyle socks, glen-plaid boxers, and blue oxford shirt, I read the love letters he'd written me. The swirls of his "Dear Anna" broke me.

Before neatly folding everything back in the box, I buried my wet face in his sweater. His scent was long gone. I pictured Samuel as I last saw him. Khaki pants and pale lavender shirt, eyes blue-green, hair the color of caramel. Beard poking through, hairline receding further on the left. Wide, thin lips.

"Be right back." His last words. I had not looked up, struggling to get a food processor and all its attachments into its box. Had his face held some shadow, some clue I might have read? If I had risen from the floor and given him a kiss, would anything have changed?

I placed my engagement ring and the money order in a sturdy envelope inside the book of female artists. Samuel and I had saved the money for our honeymoon in Barbados. I hadn't added to or subtracted from the sum since he left. I might have used the money eventually, but sad to say, I didn't yet have the enthusiasm to make any plans. And I know what it's like to struggle for money. When Samuel left, I was only twenty-one, just starting out in my work as a nurse. I didn't know if I'd be able to afford the house by myself. For the first few years I lived paycheck to paycheck, until I learned how to live with very little. Maybe the money would be enough to give the Farrells a fresh start. We all deserve one.

In the gift box I placed the art books I bought for Jen, one of my sketchpads, along with my drawing of The Roebling Suspension Bridge, showing the Ohio River converging with the Licking River. One in my series of local bridge sketches that had become synonymous with the new life Samuel and I were beginning. Holding the drawing, I thought about how my fear of bridges had melded into a fascination with them, especially this suspension bridge. Massive stone towers connected by a round arch from which a network of twisted steel cables fanned out vertically and diagonally. As a child, I'd loved the hum of tires on the bridge's mesh metal deck, and the gold-leafed finials on the towers' turrets. But the plaque with the date 1866, the year the bridge was completed, worried me when I realized how long ago that was. I touched the center of my drawing, remembering how I'd first discovered, as a teenager walking to a Cincinnati

Reds ballgame at Riverfront Stadium, the zigzag stairs winding up the side of the stone towers.

Jen found the box I'd left near their door. She released a high-pitched squeal which brought her parents onto the porch. I scooted down in the recliner and caught glimpses of them through the porch railing. They ran inside and hurried out with their remaining boxes and furniture. Alice threw armloads of grill utensils in the backseat of her car. Jack dropped a tangle of empty wire clothes hangers into the truck bed. They left an exercise bike and vacuum sweeper on the front lawn.

As Alice's car passed, she waved out the window. I could pretend she waved at me in acknowledgement, but more likely she waved good riddance to her house and that part of her life. The last I saw of the Farrells was Jen's lustrous black hair. As I grabbed my keys, headed for an art supply store, I pictured Jen's hands resting on my sketchpad. We could not wait to make our first mark on the wide-open page.

Constraints

I'm too curious for my own good. Usually it gets me in trouble. Every so often it's my saving grace.

When I walked into Dr. Metzger's waiting room, I saw a deputy jailor, and a convict wearing a dark and light gray striped jumpsuit with ankle and wrist chains. There goes my tax dollars, treating a convict's stuffy nose. I could hear my live-in boyfriend Seth saying, "Verna, keep your nose out of other people's business." I inherited nosiness from my father. He worked twenty-seven years as a Boone County policeman. No matter where he went, even when off duty, even after twenty years of retirement, he always looked for what he called "shady dealings."

For the past eighteen years, since the age of eighteen, I've processed applications for health and life insurance, verifying the truth, sniffing out lies. People lie about their weight, current health, medical history, and age. As a result, I drive Seth nuts the way I fire questions at him. He feels as if he's under interrogation. I think I'm just making conversation until I notice him getting squirrelly, and he'll say, "You're doing it again."

My family doctor referred me to Dr. Metzger for migraine headaches.

The small links of the prisoner's chains didn't look sturdy. Maybe he was only a petty criminal. Medium height, his dark brown hair clumped in tufts which stuck out every-which-way. What Seth called a bed-head, created from a sex romp followed by a cuddle-nap. Short hairs edged the convict's lips like a dirty bathtub ring. His long and fleshy nose loomed too big for his face. Seth said your nose continued to grow the older you got, but the convict didn't look any older than me—thirty-nine.

My boyfriend is a trivia junkie. Stores funky facts nobody needs to know. Some of his recent tidbits were "It's a crime in Harrisburg, Pennsylvania to have sex with a truck driver in a tollbooth; humans and horses are the only two female mammals with hymens; in Middle Eastern Islamic countries it's illegal to eat a lamb you've had sex with." My standard response to his revelations is, "And this affects me how?" But he knows I love the weird gems he chooses for me. Often they're sexual, almost always irreverent—the best kind of humor. Sometimes I believe Seth makes up his trivia to test my bullshit meter. It tickled me not to call him on it.

I knew the prisoner from somewhere. Could he be one of the endless number of applicants and policyholders I've interacted with? I prided myself on remembering names and faces, but his eluded me. Something about his eyes held the key. How fine lines fanned from the outer edges. His lids looked oily. He saw me checking him out. His leer of pleasure made my skin crawl.

The deputy jailor, seated beside him, appeared to have just come off a three-day drunk. Face pocked and red-patched, the lower half covered with stubble. His lips looked bitten and raw, but his eyes overflowed with kindness. I suspected he'd come close to wearing chains himself.

He reminded me of Dad—seventy-five and still living at home alone, but only going through the motions of life. His emphysema had worsened to the point where he refused to dress or leave the house unless forced. He depended more and more on the oxygen. Most of the day and night he spent in the leather lounger working crossword and Sudoku puzzles.

Nursing homes obsessed me for the past months—researching, compiling lists of pros and cons, constructing graphs and charts for evaluation. I asked Dad along on my scouting trips to give him input on his future home, but he refused to participate. Seth suggested letting him be. If only my younger brother Cody could help me decide. But he's a hundred miles away, incarcerated at LaGrange for being an accessory to an auto theft.

Two years of his three-year sentence remained. He claimed to be in the wrong place at the wrong time.

I tried to raise him after Mom died. Dad worked so much overtime on second and third shift that he wasn't around anymore to influence Cody. On one hand it must have rankled Dad that his own son committed a crime. At the same time, I don't believe he ever forgave himself for allowing Cody to get into trouble. I tried to keep the peace between them. Before Mom died, Dad had started a teen boy's club in our basement. They played pool, a jukebox, worked out with weights. He helped so many boys stay out of trouble. But when Mom died, it all fell apart.

"What are you here for?" the convict asked me.

I thought of coming back with, "What are you in prison for?"

His skin looked thick and weathered as if he worked outside year round. The deputy nudged him with his elbow. The prisoner was evidently supposed to keep his mouth shut.

"Cancer in the lining of my nose." I enjoyed lying on occasion.

"Sorry to hear that." His voice sounded familiar too. "I've got a deviated septum."

Bet you're a lot more deviated than just your nose, I thought. Tried not to look directly at him, but more at the picture window behind him. The sky held two wide horizontal stripes like the prisoner's jumpsuit, the top stripe a menacing purple-gray of a bruise. Beneath it was a stripe of pale blue. A ribbon of neon turquoise separated the two.

The nursing home I'd chosen called yesterday to say there was a room available for Dad. I'd put him on the waiting list eight months ago. Dad did not take the news well.

"I used to be a boxer," the convict said. "Had my nose broken one time too many."

His nose looked much too straight and smooth. No knobs or ridges.

"How interesting." I bit my tongue to keep from laughing.

Cody boxed in high school, but hadn't stuck with it anymore than the karate, lacrosse, or weight-lifting he dabbled with. I attended his games and matches, cheered him on, hoping he'd find the niche that opened up his life.

When the convict shifted in his chair, the neck of his jumpsuit slipped to reveal the top of a tattoo. It looked like tail feathers of a peacock—iridescent green, gold, and blue. I didn't object to tattoos. Thought of getting one myself. But if visible, they limited your job possibilities and pegged you as a badass. I once forbade Cody to get any tattoos, as if that would stop him. For his eighteenth birthday he got an anaconda tattoo that wound around one arm, up over his shoulder with its head resting on his chest. I didn't tell him, but it was beautiful—the rich gold and black pattern, the way it coiled and climbed. We both liked snakes, always trying to convince our parents to let us have one for a pet. When he was eleven I took him to the mall to get our picture taken with a Burmese Python. It was heavy, draped around our shoulders, its body almost as big around as Cody's head.

"I won a Golden Glove in the featherweight division two years in a row."

Who was this convict kidding? He'd never been a boxer. That would have involved training and dedication. He had a lazy streak, and always took the quick, easy way. No doubt he told this story countless times, until he believed it himself. Maybe it was the only thing in his life he could be proud of.

Seth said I judged people too harshly, before I gave them a chance to prove my first impression wrong. I expected the worst in people. As much as I hated to admit it, he's right. I blamed it on my job, where I'm paid to expose liars and cheaters. He pointed out that it's a much deeper problem. I've lost my trust in people, because of my abandonment issues, with my Mom dying when I was a teenager. Seth's a social worker and wannabe psychiatrist. I countered by saying he had savior issues. It never slid into anything nasty between us. Neither of us enjoyed fighting. He's laid back—an asset in his line of work.

The receptionist called for Derek Conrad. The prisoner rose. How could I forget those eyes? Large, greenish-blue that gazed into, not past me. Derek attended high school with me. Loners, we hung at the outskirts, on opposite sides of a large circle we couldn't make our way around or inside. In Senior English he read a poem about horses that blew me away. It reminded me of my favorite poem—James Wright's "A Blessing." Lots of boys wrote poems. Horrific dirges, anything to get laid. Derek's poem made me see, feel, and wonder. I never talked to him though we shared many imaginary conversations and encounters. He intended to join the Peace Corps, I heard. Many nights I fell asleep dreaming of accompanying him into Nicaragua, Swaziland, or Fiji where we worked side by side in schools, clinics, and fields. I lost track of Derek after high school, when Mom died and life as I knew it derailed. He lived on one of the few farms left in Erlanger, Kentucky. Where had he taken the wrong turn?

In my brother's case, it was the wrong crowd. I tried to turn him around, but what boy does what his big sister tells him? Cody was ten when Mom died. I often wondered if she'd lived and Dad hadn't gone hollow, how my brother's life would have developed.

The deputy jailor and Derek headed toward the hall to the examination rooms. He struggled to walk with the chains, lilting and shuffling side to side. As he passed, his eyes met mine. In high school they contained an intensity that threatened to break loose. Now they were flat and so dark they looked black. Maybe he'd done something innocuous, and one circumstance led to another until he found himself in a compromising position he couldn't back out of. In high school I imagined being his girlfriend and saving him. Though he'd never been in trouble, I sensed him veering further and further off-center. My love could have pulled him back.

I had the last appointment of the day, so the waiting room was empty. Solid plush chairs of deep purple alternated with emerald green, except one end held two purple in a row followed by two green. My mind kept saying the arrangement wasn't right. It needed to be consistent. Seth said I had a terrible compulsion to control things and to put things in the order I thought they belonged. He liked things messy and out of sequence. We met somewhere in the middle.

I'd moved the misplaced purple and green chairs to the center of the room when the receptionist opened the door and called my name. The woman said nothing about the condition of the waiting room. She wore a thin gold necklace with one tiny loose pearl that had slid half way round her neck. In my opinion, she'd want to know, but I heard Seth's voice saying, "See how long you can mind your own business."

"Your pearl's cockeyed," I told the receptionist.

She slid her hand along the chain until she found the errant pearl, and brought it around to the front. "Thank you." Her wide smile revealed a smudge of red lipstick on her teeth. In Seth's honor I held myself back from pointing it out. But I wanted to tell him that sometimes people needed someone to mind their business.

A nurse led me past a large inner area filled with work surfaces and filing cabinets floor to ceiling. Two women worked at computers, the third examined paperwork. Inside an examination room, the nurse took my blood pressure and told me Dr. Metzger would be with me shortly. Like hell. You could wait another forty-five minutes before the doctor came. This was just another staging area. I leaned back in my chair and closed my eyes. I'd wake when the door opened.

My mind replayed the argument with Dad earlier in the day. He'd quit taking the medicines I compiled in a clearly marked container for each day and time. After falling several times, he promised to be more careful and agreed to use a cane, but not a walker. Dad said he wanted to live on his own terms and die in his own house. He'd asked, "Doesn't any human being deserve that?"

Trite as it sounds, Dad prided himself on his role of protecting citizens. And he was good at it. Received a Valor Award, a Meritorious Award, and a Distinguished Service Award. He'd repeated the same question he asked me most mornings: "Why can't I just die, now that I've outlived my usefulness."

I asked him to tell me about the time he met Rodney Dangerfield, and when he was part of President Reagan's entourage. His spirits improved when he replayed the good times. But I also remembered the stories I never asked him to tell, the ones that hid in the shadows of the prized stories. The hostage situation that turned fatal, when he made a decision he never forgave himself for.

I heard the doctor's voice in the adjoining room, but couldn't distinguish his words, so I moved to the shared wall, and leaned my ear against it. Dr Metzger said he'd let the numbing medication work for a while. Chills ran up my arms as I heard the clank of Derek's chains. I got back in my chair seconds before Dr. Metzger entered the room. He examined the interior of my nose with a lighted instrument, and said, "I don't see any polyps."

The doctor looked young enough to be my son. Lately too damn many adults were young enough to be my children. Even though I have none. I loved living with Seth, but wasn't sure either of us would make good parents.

"You have very large turbinates." His voice insinuated it was shameful to have turbinates the size of mine. I'm not petite. My turbinates are no doubt perfectly sized for my body. The doctor showed me a diagram of the nose, pointed to sacs along each side, extending into the cheeks. "With surgery, I can trim your turbinates back some. You'll have less trouble with sinus infections, allergies, and possibly migraines. But we'll want to have an MRI of your sinuses done."

The doctor said he needed to check my nasal passages. He stuck a sprayer up each nostril and released the numbing agent. A horrible taste bloomed in my mouth. He fidgeted with instruments in the corner. I heard a loud noise from what sounded like the room next door. A heavy thud vibrated my chair.

"Was that thunder?" I asked.

"Hmm?" He eyed me over top of tiny metal-framed glasses. "Now open wide."

He squirted a solution down my throat. "This will be even worse."

He was right.

"Tastes like dirt, doesn't it?" He seemed pleased. "Now we'll let that numb up a while. I'll be right back."

Within seconds of when he left the room, my throat felt as if it was swelling shut. I'd never had my throat numbed. Maybe this was a normal sensation. I tried to relax and breathe slow, deep breaths. Again I heard a loud noise from the room I suspected Derek and the deputy occupied. A sound like a ripe melon hurled against concrete was followed by a floor-shaking thud. I lunged out of the examination chair and grabbed the doorknob.

Derek hobbled in the hallway, his forehead bloody, a stream trickling into his eyes. Before I had time to evaluate the situation, I tripped him. He fell full force, smacking the carpet face down with a crunch that could only mean broken bones.

"Call 911 and Security," I screamed.

I pressed my foot hard on Derek's upper back, thinking Dad would be proud. Derek didn't budge, but I saw the up and down motion of his lungs.

I yelled that I couldn't breathe. One nurse got on the phone, another rushed to my side. She explained that the numbing solution only made my throat feel like it was closing. If I didn't relax and take deep, slow breaths, I'd make it worse.

A third woman ran to check on Dr. Metzger and the deputy jailor. Derek had evidently butted heads with them, knocking each out, somehow having enough adrenalin and desperation to stay conscious long enough to stumble into the hallway.

A nurse brought me a portable oxygen mask, but by that time I was breathing freely. Two security guards arrived as Derek revived and began to writhe. Two men strong-armed him into a chair. He no longer struggled. There was nowhere to go.

I'll never forget the look in his eyes, right before I tripped him. He believed he had a chance. Who knows how far he could have gone? Maybe his friends waited round the corner in a van with a hacksaw to remove his chains. Maybe he would have mended his ways. This might have been his first crime, not one in a long string of offenses. Like my brother, maybe he'd been in the wrong place at the wrong time. Sometimes it was that simple. Everyone deserved a second chance.

The guards shackled him. While the nurses tended to the deputy jailor and Dr. Metzger, I found a stack of sterile gauze pads. I wet them with a wound spray. Derek's eyes held the same trapped look as Dad's when I told him the nursing home had a place ready for him. The same look in my brother's eyes the last time I visited him in jail six months ago. I couldn't stand the fact that I'd failed to save Cody. What were the chances prison could rehabilitate him? Would he have to lie from now on about his incarceration in order to get a job, find a place to live, or have any hopes of a relationship?

I gently cleansed Derek's face, whispering "I'm sorry," as tears ran down my cheeks.

He kept his eyes averted. I couldn't tell if he knew I'd tripped him, or if he thought he'd blacked out. He never recognized me.

I left Dr. Metzger's office with more than my throat numb. Walking around the square for over an hour, as Seth says, "Letting the stink blow off me." I thought about my last visit with Cody. He said he'd taken up chess with a group of inmates. It changed his life. Slowed him down, made him think before acting. I couldn't picture chess in prison, but I wanted to believe my brother. He looked so rough—his face scratched, a black and blue eye. Getting into fistfights was a hobby of Cody's.

I used my cell phone to call Seth and asked, "What do you think about renting an apartment down the street from Dad?"

"You know I don't care where we live."

He grew up in a trailer park. Our studio apartment seemed spacious to him.

"Why not let Dad stay in his house, and die there if he wants to?"

"Sounds like a plan." Seth didn't mention that he'd suggested the idea to me six months ago.

"I've been thinking about learning to play chess."

"I'd love to teach you."

He met a group of college friends monthly to play. For years he'd urged me to learn.

"We're due for a weekend away," he said. "Haven't been in the woods for weeks. How about we rent a cabin at Red River Gorge, and afterwards swing west and visit Cody? I miss him."

Seth had been wearing me down for some time, hinting we take a ride down to LaGrange. But he never rubbed in the fact that I'd abandoned my brother. Seth liked to tease me, but he never turned mean.

"Verna, what do you say I make your favorite supper tonight? Tomato basil soup and my special dill grilled cheese. I'll have it ready by the time you get home."

We talked for a few more minutes. He revealed his latest trivia nuggets: "Stewardesses is the longest word that is typed with only the left hand," and "An eyelash lives for only five months."

I hung up the phone, thinking how much Seth's voice soothed me. And wishing I'd let Derek escape.

Taking Count

I saw Shay every weekday on my walk to and from Covington Animal Hospital, where I worked as a veterinarian's assistant. He lived in an older house on Garrard Street in a rundown section of Covington, one of the few city homes with a spacious side yard. Room enough for a patio with umbrella table, chairs, and an extensive garden. He was born in Jamaica. Well over six feet tall, limbs thick and muscled, skin that gleamed. I would never have guessed leukemia spiraled through him.

My job paid minimum wage, but was the only job I'd held for longer than three months. Every other week Dr. Wilkins tried to match me up with one of his nephews, cousins, friends' sons, or single men whose pets he treated. More than once I overheard phone conversations in which the doctor described me as petite, with long straight blond hair and blue-gray eyes; sweet, a little shy, loves animals. Was that all I added up to?

I could have told him to say that I had a straight, unobtrusive nose and small ears with heart-shaped lobes, that I loved art and anything tiny. But I replied that I wasn't dating at the moment. Eventually I lied, saying I was already seeing someone. Dr. Wilkins told me I was a born natural at taking care of things. He accepted a lot of charity cases and strays. That explained the reason he hired me.

Doctors had diagnosed me with OCD in my late teens. My main ob-session was counting: my steps, number of bites I took, sycamores, calico cats, skunks, crows; tabulating running totals summarized by day, week, month, year, century, and lifetime. All things mathematical intrigued me. I loved to solve equations and work with fractions, decimals, and progres-sions. The way things added up, how they balanced, the relationship of parts to a whole fascinated me.

I turned the corner onto Shay's street at seven minutes after seven. When I was two houses away, he came onto his porch, broom in hand. He was a sweeper. Brushed off his porch, sidewalk, and patio. Moved every-thing over the curb and down into the street where it became the respon-sibility of street cleaners. For the past month I'd walked past his house. Garrard Street ran long and straight, giving me a while to watch him. Peo-ple didn't sweep outside much anymore. They owned blowers that did the dirty work. If I ran across a sweeper, they were usually female, and most often elderly, but Shay looked as natural sweeping as if he'd been born with a broom in his hand.

Normally I walked to and from work on Scott Street, perpendicular to the Ohio River. But since spring had warmed and softened the earth, the water company had begun digging trenches in the street and sidewalk for several blocks. I hated the detour onto Garrard, until I saw Shay.

We spoke a few words as I passed the first week—morning, noon, and dusk. More the second, third, and fourth weeks. I complimented his garden, wished him a good day. With each pass the number of words ex-changed increased exponentially. They reached critical mass on the sev-enth of June. When I passed Shay at noon, on my way to pick up oxtail soup and grilled cheese sandwiches for Dr. Wilkins' and my lunch, I made a decision. On my return trip I would ask Shay to have dinner with me that evening. His smile warmed me all the way to Wertheim's Deli. I didn't count anything until I crossed Fifth Street, six blocks from Shay's house. My stomach felt like the bowls I held—soup sloshing back and forth as I walked. How could I ask him? What if he declined? Accepted?

I counted my number of steps from the curb of Seventh to Eighth, from the old Coppin Building to what used to be Woolworth's, the Brad-ford pear tree to the star maple. If any interval ended on an odd number, I would not invite him to dinner. They all ended even.

When I asked, Shay's face lit up momentarily. "I don't eat out much." He did not resume sweeping, but waited at his iron gate. No fence, just a gate, sturdy and ornate. I counted the number of finials, rods of grillwork, and spiral sections.

"My treat. I got a raise today," I lied. "What about a cheese ravioli dinner from Germantown?"

He asked if I'd split one with him. He couldn't eat much. When I returned that night, he had changed from the T-shirt and shorts of that morning to a collared knit shirt and khaki pants. I counted the tiny pale blue and yellow diamonds of his shirt. He'd set his umbrella table with red-and-white checkered placemats, coordinating cloth napkins, and two mismatched china plates. An intricate black and white lace pattern decorated my plate. His contained a maroon cityscape against a cream background. Crystal goblets, candlesticks, and silver utensils completed the setting. I usually ate off paper plates and drank out of a plastic McDonald's cup.

Shay lit the white tapers. Though it wasn't anywhere near dark, tall overhanging trees and close neighboring houses created deep shade. A small milk glass vase held fragrant honeysuckle, sweet peas, yellow roses, and basil.

I reintroduced myself with an exaggerated accent. "I'm Savannah. And no I'm not from the South."

His smile revealed straight teeth, lustrous as pearls. He wore thin gold-framed glasses. His head was bald and he looked odd without eyebrows and eyelashes.

Shay took tiny bites and chewed each for a long time before swallowing. When I spoke, he leaned in to listen. He didn't yet know my counting obsession, so I concentrated on not moving my lips when I tallied the strawberries painted on the umbrella, the number of bricks visible on his house.

"I love fruit," he said. "Especially mango, guava, papaya, pomegranate. We'll have some star apple for dessert." His eyes were deep-set and shiny as hematite.

He asked where I lived. I described the apartment on the top floor of The Phelps, across from Lytle Park in downtown Cincinnati, where I house-sat for a professor while he and his wife lived in Crete for a year sabbatical. I'd never owned a place of my own, always lived in other people's houses. My clothes and shoes filled one suitcase and my life's work (notebooks crammed with tabulations and calculations) in another. A third held my miniatures bubble-wrapped. I didn't need furniture, household goods, books, music, or pets. They were furnished for me, to watch over and use. I took good care of other people's belongings.

"Do you own a car?" he asked. "You're always walking."

I explained that I walked and rode a bus for safety—others' and mine. I owned a car once, a red Rambler, for twenty days. I couldn't concentrate on driving when there was so much to count. Cars (by make and color), trees (by genus and species), houses (brick vs. siding, vs. frame), pedestrians (male vs. female). I wrecked the car three times.

He told me he had lost his job and car as a result of his leukemia. His wife of five years left him. She could no longer handle the fear and uncertainty of his illness. She wanted children and stability. He could provide neither.

I couldn't believe we were talking about such intimate things. The strain in his voice made me want to count the goldfinches, grackles, and chickadees in his yard. But with birds, you can never be sure you haven't counted them more than once. I can't tolerate inaccuracy.

Since I'd never heard of star fruit, he brought a plate and a sharp knife outside to show me how to cut it. First he trimmed the brown edge from each of the five ridges that made up the star points, then he turned the waxy yellow cylinder on its side before slicing thin cross-sections of stars. He arranged them in large, shallow china bowls with chipped rims, patterned with tiny lilies-of-the-valley. The fruit's crisp texture reminded me of a Braeburn apple—sweet and crisp with a tart edge.

"Why do you sweep?" I asked.

"It keeps me sane."

Most people might not understand. "With me, it's numbers. I live to count."

He leaned and touched the broom handle resting against his house. "It's all I have left of my mother."

Her only income was from making brooms after his father died when Shay was five.

She couldn't work her fingers fast enough to fill the orders. Taught him to sweep at the age of eight with a special broom she made to match his height. She believed sweeping akin to prayer. Told him she'd fit through many a tight spot, worked out many a knot in her gut, healed many a wound in her heart by sweeping. Said it reminded her of rocking him in her arms.

His voice contained such joy and sorrow. How I envied their relationship. I didn't even know my birth mother's name.

Shay handed me the broom. The pads of his fingers had worn the handle shiny. He rose without another word, and went inside. He looked unsteady on his feet. I squinted to see past his back door, but could only discern an opening that must lead to the basement. A network of six gnarled cacti and nine succulents, mostly dried carcasses, obscured the two windows. I turned to face his lush yard: a grape arbor, rose garden, herb garden, cutting garden and vegetable plot. Four mimosas, two cottonwoods, one each of tulip poplar, sweet gum, pin oak, and catalpa formed the perimeter of his side yard. The interior held smaller ones: fringe tree, hawthorn, and smoke tree. I thought of counting low-growing vs. tall plants, tabulating the colors. I was worried about Shay.

He returned, carrying a smaller broom. "Stand up. I'll show you."

From behind he encircled me with his arms, and gave me the broom. His shaking hands covered mine. His skin felt like the soft underside of a puppy's ear. He smelled like coconut. Later he revealed his use of the sweet oil to camouflage the chemo's metallic odor and counteract its effect on his skin. He told me very little about his leukemia. I wanted to know more, but honored his reticence.

"Like so." He swung the broom for me, removing his hands after I learned the progression. "It's all in the shoulders and wrists. Lean into it. Don't sway the broom. Let it lead you. Take your time. There'll always be something to sweep."

I worked toward the street, struggling not to count my broom strokes.

"Yes, that's it. You're finding your rhythm."

He came around in front of me, looked up and down my length. "I was your height when I was eight. This should fit you." Again he placed his hands over mine on the handle.

"I'd like you to have this broom."

I'd never received such a gift, nor given one. His hands remained, warming mine. I didn't dare lift my eyes to his, or speak. In and out I breathed while counting the diamonds woven into the pattern of his pullover.

"Savannah, may you always sweep well." His voice was soft and thick as syrup.

Every nerve ending prickled. I wanted to count something—the lines of his hands, the rings of his knuckles, the joints of his fingers.

He stiffened and sat down hard, his face lowered. I didn't understand why he seemed embarrassed that I'd seen him in pain, but I thanked him for a wonderful evening, and said I needed to get home. Thoughts of Shay kept interrupting my counts on the way. I neared the Roebling Suspension Bridge across the Ohio River, and began as always to tally its blue braided steel cables.

A few days later Shay asked me to have dinner with him. He fixed some of his mother's favorite Jamaican recipes: cream of pumpkin soup, vegetable rundown, sweet cassava pudding, and hibiscus iced tea. I'm not a venturous eater, so I was afraid I'd hurt his feelings if I couldn't eat what he'd taken so much time to prepare. But everything tasted delicious. He'd Americanized them just a bit, mostly tamed down the spices. I asked what kinds of fruits grew in Jamaica. He described ackee, naseberry, tamarind, and stinking toe. The color and depth of his eyes intensified as he talked about the flowers and trees he missed: lobster-claw, jacaranda, Poinciana. I wondered why he hadn't returned once divorced, once he'd found out about his leukemia.

After dinner he asked me to tell him the story of my life. I told how I went from foster home to foster home until a couple adopted me. Afraid they'd send me back, I hid a lot of my compulsive behaviors from my adoptive parents. I recounted my troubles in school, my inability to concentrate on anything but counting, how I'd never kept jobs long. If I was typing, I counted letters, words, paragraphs; verbs, nouns, adverbs, adjectives; vowels vs. consonants. I reveled in the relationships of measurement— length vs. width, height vs. depth. My idea of fun involved solving equations, developing formulas, recording and analyzing sequences of numbers. I spoke of my latest preoccupation, The Divine Proportion, found in art, music, nature, DNA, the solar system, the Pyramids, and the human body. Using one of his sunflowers I described how every seed head grew in an ever-expanding spiral pattern of fifty-five clockwise seeds followed by eighty-nine counterclockwise, growing from the center out, packing the seeds in the most efficient angle.

I told Shay about my one extravagance—that I collected objects an inch or smaller. Things like a rose quartz seahorse, agate marble, jasper tortoise, pewter windmill, cloisonné peacock, porcelain panther, and hematite heart. From my pant's pocket I pulled my tiny white horse with black patches.

"This was my first one. I found it when I was only eight, in an abandoned flower bed." When I held it in the palm of my hand, I felt how vibrant horses were, the energy they generated when they ran.

He asked if I carried the horse with me every day.

"Not always him. I pick a different miniature each morning, like putting on a pair of earrings before you leave the house."

He laughed in deep fully-felt tones that made me want to join in. "Why?"

"They're my hidden good luck charms. Anytime of the day, I can hold them in my pocket with no one the wiser. Or I can bring them out, look at them."

I balanced the horse standing erect in the palm of my hand. He touched the curve of the horse's head.

"It makes me happy to look at something so tiny, so contained." I leaned the horse against the umbrella pole.

When he asked where I found them, I said everywhere—at the beach, underneath bushes, in parking lots, antique shops, toy stores, flea markets, on the Internet."

"How many do you have?"

"They're the only thing I don't count. And I give them away."

I described how I'd recently joined an online club of miniature collectors. Randomly, we mailed a member a piece from our collection and when that person received it, they reciprocated with one of theirs. They're only loaned. At some point, one of the exchangees returned their loaned piece and when the loaner received it, they followed suit and mailed the other's back.

"How cool," he said. "So you never know when you'll receive one, or when you'll get yours returned?"

"Exactly." I told him how the club members never met, their only contact was to receive and give miniatures by randomly selecting names and addresses from the website.

"Like a secret society." When he grinned, the skin of his forehead furrowed like waves upon a shore. "But aren't you worried you'll lose your favorite pieces?"

"I've never lost one yet. They always come back. It was hard to send them out when I first joined. But now I love to mail my most treasured ones."

I tried to explain how scary and yet exhilarating it was to let them go. But I never gave up my horse. He was my cornerstone.

Shay looked directly into my eyes while I spoke, disconcerting at first. But they held such candor and compassion it became easier to meet them. I described the homes I watched over the years. He needed words, not so much their meaning, but their sound and flow. When he stiffened, or pressed his lips together tight against the pain, I talked faster, inventing things to make the stories longer, funnier.

"I don't want to keep you if you need to be somewhere," he said.

"No, I left enough food out for Brutus, the cat where I'm house-sitting. He's big, fat, and yellow."

I described the west and south view of the city from my apartment. The kitchen faced the old Guilford School, Lytle Park, the Ohio River, Kentucky. A little balcony off the living room looked uptown, giving me a birds-eye view of Christ Church Cathedral—twenty spires, fourteen turrets, thirty-one finials, and forty-seven arched windows lit from within.

"What would you like to count now?"

"Maybe the number of times you've blinked your eyes, scratched your arm, or touched the tabletop."

"How can you do all that counting and talk at the same time? Can't you use that in some business way; turn your curse into a blessing?"

"I haven't found a way. It's the odd things I want to count, things there's no good reason to."

Silence fell, surprisingly comfortable. Dusk settled around us. Eleven crows congregated in his neighbor's sycamore, chattering like a clutch of women gossiping.

I asked what kind of work he did. Painting houses, he said, but painting canvases was his passion. "Anything that has to do with color makes me happy. My mother encouraged me to paint. She believed color had the power to heal."

He said he spent hours looking at color wheels, studying gradations and intensities. Color relaxed and grounded him, the same as sweeping. His mother insisted he attend college in the United States. She'd saved a considerable amount of her income from broom making, but he'd received a full scholarship to The University of Cincinnati's Art Academy. There he met his wife, Camelia. His voice, sounding her beautiful name, fell like a stone through water.

I asked a question about his herb garden, to distract him. He said his mother swore by remedies using herbs such as arrowroot, bissy nut, chainy root, spirit weed, and shame-a-macka.

"She even had an elixir for a broken heart," he said."You make a tea by steeping yarrow, bay leaves, borage, lavender, and basil with a dab of honey. I can't say it works."

I responded without thinking. "I've never been in love."

Shay sang me a slow, sweet lament his mother used to sing. She never revealed what the words meant. They sounded more like keening than actual words.

We talked while darkness gathered, until bugs began to bite. Shay said he hated for me to walk home in the dark, and asked if I could catch a bus. I replied that the number eighteen bus brought me between twenty-two and twenty-seven steps from the Phelps. He walked me to his wrought iron gate.

I didn't take the bus. For years I've walked in the dark. No one's ever bothered me. Maybe all my numbers wove a web around me that others couldn't break.

We spent many evenings together. Sometimes he'd invite me; other times I'd invite myself. Our lives entwined like the spearmint and snow-on-the-mountain in his garden. We made a pact. When together, no counting and no sweeping. We slipped up sometimes. He'd pick up the broom propped against his house, and take one or two strokes before he realized what he'd done. Or I'd find myself mouthing a number before comprehending I'd counted the notes of St. Ben's bells. Sometimes he rushed inside to hide the fact that he couldn't keep food down. Every day I brought him a few cans of Ensure. He always thanked me and wanted to pay for them, but I'm not sure he drank them. Each visit I brought a different miniature to show him. As he'd hold it in his open palm, I'd tell where I found it, and why I kept it, before returning it to the depths of my pocket.

We had our rituals. When I first arrived, he walked me through his garden, pointed out newly bloomed perennials, annuals that had reseeded. One night he ruffled the pale green and cream-edged pineapple mint, and raised his fingers to my nose.

"See how good it smells?"

I cupped his hand and inhaled. His warm skin smelled of pineapple, coconut, the sun and the sea. "Look how large your hand is compared to mine."

He looked at his palm as if I'd shown him something he'd never seen. "I believe it's the exact size of your cheek."

I closed my eyes as he touched his palm to my face. Against his hand, I flicked my tongue.

He withdrew. "Quite the little cat."

I asked if Shay liked cats. He questioned why I wanted to know, a suspicious look on his face. I told him about the skinny cat I found by the back door at the animal hospital. I named her Maggie the Cat after one of my favorite movies, *Cat on a Hot Tin Roof*. Dr. Wilkins said he'd have to put her to sleep if no one claimed her. Shay couldn't say whether he liked cats or not. He'd never owned a pet. Nor had I.

For two weeks I seeded Shay with details and anecdotes about Maggie the Cat, until I arrived with her in a carrier and a bag of food.

"I wondered when she'd show up," he said.

"She can stay outside."

"She'll tear up my garden."

"And keep mice away."

I sat the carrier on the patio. Shay opened the door and Maggie slinked out. They connected quickly. I knew they would. I'd lied about Dr. Wilkins possibly putting her to sleep.

Mornings when I passed, Shay'd be sweeping, Maggie'd be trying to understand the broom's motion before pouncing on the straws. He gently swept the cat out of his way.

I never learned Shay's age. He was five years older than me, I decided, making him thirty-four. His mother had died a few years earlier. I asked if he had any pictures of her. He placed his hand over his heart. "Only here."

He tried to hide the fact that he couldn't eat any more by cutting food up and moving it around the plate. Part of me wanted to force the issue, demand he eat, ask was he trying to starve himself to death. I began watching his face more closely while we ate, and realized either the way food looked or smelled sickened him. But he seemed to enjoy watching me eat.

The bones of his skull and face had become so prominent it hurt me to look at him, so I concentrated on his dark eyes. But even they'd turned distant in the past week, as if he existed half in this world, half in the next. More than once he'd drifted away—eyes open but clearly in an altered state. I pretended not to notice, continuing with my story or petting Maggie, counting down the seconds.

Near the end of the summer he invited me inside his house for the first time. Judging by the dead plants in the windows, I expected his interior to look run down and dreary. I assumed he was ashamed of me seeing it.

"I told you I love color," he warned, switching on the kitchen light.

He'd painted the walls and ceiling graduated shades of tangerine, mango, apricot; the windows and doorframes rich terra cotta. I pictured him on a beach with the sun gleaming his skin. He walked me through his rooms, each a study of color. Several times he stopped and stood still. I waited close behind him, praying he didn't fall. He tried to hide the fact that he needed to steady himself against the walls as we walked.

His furnishings were sparse and simple in crisp shades of violet, fuchsia, turquoise and lime—solids everywhere, not a stripe, plaid, or floral to be found. From the bedroom closet he pulled his canvases: children building a mud dam across a creek, goldfinches in a puddle, a snake sunning on a flat river rock, and a woman climbing a tree with heart-shaped leaves the size of her face. "Blue Mahoe," he said. "The only place in the world they grow is Jamaica and Cuba."

"Why don't you hang these? They need to be seen."

"By whom?"

I was sorry I asked, but wondered if he'd ever exhibited his paintings. How I wanted one for myself. No, I wanted them all, to look into over and over again. He used vibrant colors in unusual pairings, and he left something slightly askew in the proportions between live and inanimate objects. The calculated incongruities rendered his work perfect.

"Here's my latest." He showed me charcoal studies of winter trees, and traced the outline of bark. "Look at the framework. The skeleton that is in no way dead." The painting detailed the intricate network above and below ground, how the roots balanced the crown.

Shay motioned toward his paintings. "These are all yours."

Unable to speak, I picked up a small canvas of sun transformed through an old, thick window. Molten-gold on a coral carpet. Its beauty soothed me.

Back outside, petting the cat in his lap, he told me his latest round of treatments had been unsuccessful. "There is nothing ..." More and more often, he stopped mid-sentence with fingers sunk in Maggie's neck fur. I pretended not to see his pain, launching into comments about his work and suggesting he teach me to paint.

"Savannah?" He always pronounced my name in a way I'd never heard it said before, elongating the vowels, emphasizing the wrong syllable, until it sounded like an exotic bird or rare orchid. "I have a week or two left."

I needed to count. Though I wanted to look away, I held his gaze. A few of his eyebrow hairs had grown back like strings of honey. He'd lost weight over the summer and his muscled arms had softened to ropes. I'd begun sweeping for him.

His oncologist advised him to go into hospice. I heard his words, but couldn't believe someone still so alive could be that close to death.

"My mother visited me in a dream last night," Shay said. "She handed me a broom, and held her warm hands over mine on the handle. The way she did when she first taught me to sweep."

"How lucky you are. My dreams are nothing but an endless parade of things to count."

"Will you take care of Maggie and my house?" He turned toward his garden, but it looked as if he saw another time and place.

I counted the bricks behind him, the strawberries on the umbrella, the seconds I felt ticking through me.

"I want it settled." He placed his hand over mine.

He'd already told me he had no living relatives, and that his will left everything to me. I tried to swallow the lump in my throat. Did I want the responsibility of ownership?

Finally I said, "Taking care of things is what I do."

He sat Maggie the Cat in my lap, went inside, and returned with a mango and something that looked like a moldy grapefruit, plates, cloth napkins, his camera, and a knife. He sliced the mango while he explained that the strange globe was called an ugli, a grapefruit and tangerine hybrid that many years ago was found growing wild in Jamaica. His hands shook as he peeled off the lumpy, loose skin and separated the inside segments like an orange. They tasted exquisitely sweet with just a touch of tang. He bit off the end of a segment and sucked the juice from it, keeping his eyes closed a long time, his lips squeezed tight. I caught myself counting the number of diamonds in the metal grid tabletop, the lime wedges on the placemats, the paisley swirls of his shirt. His fingers moved over the surface of the mango, past patches of gold, yellow, red and green. He said he'd decided to save the mango for his morning smoothie. In a Vitamixer he concocted the best blends of pomegranate, pineapple, and papaya juices.

Shay snapped pictures of Maggie licking the empty ugli rind, and of me rocking her like an infant in my arms. He set up his tripod and captured poses of me, him, and Maggie the Cat. I snapped photos of Shay kneeling in his garden (I had to help him up and down), beneath his mimosa tree staring up to the sky through its branches.

He removed a tiny box from his pants pocket and handed it to me. I opened it to find a miniature pen and ink sketch of Maggie the Cat splayed out in the grass.

"Something for your collection."

I couldn't believe how he'd compressed so much intricate detail onto such a small area. I reached inside my shirt pocket, enfolded the miniature spotted horse in my hand, and brought it out. After looking at it one more time, I took a deep breath, and extended it to Shay.

"I'd like to give you my horse." I placed it in his palm.

"Are you sure?"

I nodded yes. "It will be your good luck charm."

He rubbed the horse's belly, saying it looked like one of the wild ponies on Assateague Island, that eat salt marsh grass which causes them to drink excessive water, giving their bellies a bloated look. He and his wife had visited the barrier island off the coast of Virginia and Maryland on his honeymoon.

Shay touched the horse's mane before slipping it into his breast pocket.

It was eleven forty-five. I didn't want the evening to end. I could have sat all night talking, listening, laughing under the stars and sliver of moon. The sweet, autumn clematis glutted the air. Maggie alternated between his lap and mine, purring as we pet her. How I wished we could freeze our remaining moments together.

He handed me a bag of red peppers he'd picked. "Probably the last bunch for this year. The cooler weather's slowed them down."

I opened the paper bag to release their essence.

"Sweet," he whispered. "Like you."

I hugged one arm around his waist. It felt as if our bodies hummed. He cradled my head, his fingertips tickling the lobe of my ear. When he began to shake, I helped him to his chair at the umbrella table. Maggie leaped into his lap. He repeated that he needed sleep. I asked if he'd let me stay the night.

"Maybe tomorrow."

"Can I help you inside?"

"I want to nap here under the stars awhile."

I patted Maggie's head, kissed Shay's crown, and made myself walk away from the table, past his mother's broom, toward the street. He remained seated.

Outside the gate, I turned back to wave. The knife glinted alongside his hand.

Shivers coursed through me. I hugged the bag of peppers against my chest. Imagined the sun warming their skin and Shay's hands as he'd held them. It would take twelve steps, six to eight seconds to reach him. But he'd made it clear he wanted me to leave. Couldn't I respect his wish?

As I headed for the corner, I reached into my pocket to touch the tiny box that nestled Shay's sketch. I tabulated the number of front porch steps and streetlights as I walked north toward the suspension bridge, envisioning my miniature horse nuzzling Shay's chest, and a matching feral horse galloping along a Jamaican bay.

What to Leave Behind

We were having sex in the kitchen, our breaths loud and ragged, everything coming together in a paisley swirl of purple and green. The sound of a garage door shimmying open was followed by the roar of a car engine. I didn't become alarmed until I realized the high heels clacking cement were coming nearer.

Roger was so close he didn't hear anything. I rose on my elbows and whisper-screamed his name. The change in angle spiked the intensity along with the rush of adrenalin at the prospect of being discovered.

The tap of heels ceased, replaced by the sound of a door handle jiggling. The door to the kitchen, ten feet away. A woman's voice called, "Roger?"

He pulled out. "Coming."

I ran on tiptoes to the bedroom. He opened the closet, whispered, "Get in. I'll get rid of her." Tossed me my bunched-up clothes before sliding the door closed.

Luckily, I've never been claustrophobic. I liked small spaces with well-delineated boundaries that made it clear how far to push the envelope. And I've never been afraid of the dark's velvet lap.

His bare feet padded onto the kitchen linoleum. Was he throwing on his clothes? Surely he wouldn't answer the door naked. A latch slid open.

I couldn't decipher what his wife Lydia said, but Roger boomed, "I was on my way into the shower. What are you doing home?" His voice dripped guilt.

My heart raced. Things like this only happened on TV.

"My class was canceled," she said. "The professor didn't show up." Her tongue lingered over the syllables as if they were Belgian truffles. She had a hint of an accent. Roger hoarded information about her. He hadn't told me that she was foreign or that she was attending college. Probably something to kill time, like Fencing, Origami, or Stargazing 101. I'd saved for years and still didn't have enough money to apply to the Fashion Design School at The University of Cincinnati. I could take out student loans, but the idea of owing large sums of money nauseated me.

Their voices neared.

"Probably busy screwing one of his students." The lilting, slightly askew way she said "screwing" made me want to see how her mouth formed the word. I pictured liquid silk.

"The man we saw in Perkins? That old geezer?" His laugh barely held back hysteria.

She said the professor, an intelligent and charismatic man, wasn't much older than Roger. I could feel him bristling.

"Isn't he married?" His voice shrill as if this was a personal affront.

"Never stopped anyone before." She sounded way too nonchalant. Maybe involved in an affair of her own. Wouldn't that send Roger reeling?

Shoes, and what felt like boxes, covered the floor of the closet. No room to stand. I'd only had seconds to find the least uncomfortable way to sit bare-bottomed before they walked into the bedroom. Threads of light from the window across the room filtered through the louvers on the closet doors. My nose tingled from the musk of dust and worn clothes. No, you are not sneezing, I told myself.

I was on Lydia's side of the closet. Hems of blazers, dresses, skirts, and pant legs brushed the top of my head. I reached to feel the linen, wool, cashmere. Nicer fabrics than I could afford.

Roger and I met in Borders Books eight months ago. He'd asked if it was okay to sit at the table where I was reading. The drape of his black silk shirt over the curve of his shoulders drew me in. His sandy hair hung in a pleasing tousled style. I suspected it matched the density of broadcloth. He sat across from me, one hand arranged alongside *The Fate of Liberty: Abraham Lincoln and Civil Liberties,* wedding ring in plain sight. I couldn't take my eyes off his long, thick fingers.

I asked about his book. He followed suit, glancing at my pile of the latest fashion design books and magazines. His teeth were straight, professionally whitened. Money, I thought, or he's in sales. Both turned out to be true. When I asked if he wanted a cup of coffee, nodding toward the coffee counter, he accepted. His lips curled suggestively.

A month ago he asked me to accompany him to a Civil War reenactment in Gettysburg. Lydia didn't want to go. Why he chose to reveal that crumb of information I'll never know. He hinted we could make a weekend of it. I said I had to work. At times I rebelled against my assumed role as runner-up. He narrowed his eyes, as if squeezing the hard edge of my lie.

I worked as a sales associate in women's casual wear at Dillard's department store, where I hoped to become a buyer. All day I handled clothes I couldn't afford, studying their cut, color, weight, sheen, texture. On my lunch break I either sketched my own designs or visited a sewing store and fingered fabrics.

I was perfectly happy that Roger was married. I wanted a sexual partner, not someone to crowd my life.

"Let's go out to eat," Roger said to Lydia. "I'm starving."

"I need a nap. Just a half hour." Her voice oozed money. Smooth and reliant. I'd seen a photo of them taken by Arturo Cabada who was sinfully expensive. Her dark blonde hair looked professionally highlighted, her makeup flawless, probably Dior. She was what I'd call pathologically thin. Occasionally Roger made comments about her, not all derogatory. Her parents were wealthy. She was spoiled.

"I'll jump in the shower," Roger said. "While you're sleeping."

"Why don't you lie down here with me?"

Somebody had a foot odor problem. I assumed the funky smell emanated from Lydia's shoes, since I was on her side of the closet. Her perfume emanated from her clothes. My Insolence? Rumeur? Pure Poison? Roger insisted I not wear any perfume, and not smoke when we rendezvoused, as he called it. Lydia had the nose of a bloodhound.

A tickle started in my nose, precursor to a sneeze. I closed my eyes tight, held my breath, and talked myself out of it. Leaning forward, I peeked out of the slit between the closet door and the wall. His gnarly toes came into view with their tiny tufts of hair that he liked to scuff against the back of my calves.

He repeated that he really needed a shower.

"I like you stinky." I imagined the way the edges of her teeth touched with the "t."

Bedsprings creaked. "Come on," she insisted, her voice fluid as velvet. "Lie down here with me."

He hesitated, as though he heard my mouthed warning, "Don't do it," but additional creaks confirmed he'd joined her. What choice did he have?

If I stood, the angle of the slats might allow me to watch them on the bed. Not that I wanted to.

"Mm, that's nice," she purred.

Filmy sounds like a series of kisses down her back. Lydia's skin no doubt luxuriously soft, pampered by expensive creams and lavish spa treatments. Silence. I closed my eyes to concentrate better. Had they fallen asleep that quick, or was something else starting up? I wanted to scream, "Can't you smell me on him, you stupid bitch?"

I wasn't worried about getting caught. What could she do to me? It would be the end of my affair with her husband, but maybe our time together had run its course. We had nothing in common, other than a strong sexual appetite. Never dined in a restaurant, saw a movie or play, hiked or took a ride in the country together. We'd shared a bottle of cloyingly sweet wine once. Definitely not a brand Lydia chose.

Some things about him had been getting on my nerves lately. How he mocked my obsession with texture—how I had to touch everything. The goofy way he said hello, dragging out the syllables in a high pitch, followed by laughter as if he'd told the funniest joke ever. The way gravity slackened his jaws and chin when beneath me in bed. He was thirty-eight, sixteen years my senior.

The thing I liked most about him was his clothes. The Lagerfeld camel hair sports coat, the silk Tommy Bahama shirt with a phoenix rising from flames, and the Ungaro safari jacket with extensive pockets and leather trim. He told me it cost $1,200. I hoped some day to design clothes for people like Roger.

They snored. Hers the swish of corduroy pant legs against each other; his the whine of cotton rending. I could sneak out of the closet into the living room, dress and slip out the back. But I wasn't ready to leave.

To my right a purse hung from a hook. The current fashionable shape—wide and not very tall, with a short strap. It felt like a crocodile's raised, segmented texture. I thumbed the catch open. I felt along the suede lining, shivering with the image of reaching into a cavern webbed with spiders. The interior held nothing. I slowly unzipped the hidden pocket. The whiz of metal teeth thrummed my fingertips. My fingers found an inch-high wad of dollars. The rustle of crisp bills reminded me of how a Vogue pattern sounded when I unfolded it for the first time, smoothed out the folds against the crosshatch of crisp linen. Couldn't decipher the bills' denomination, but suspected at least twenties. Plumbing the inner pocket's contours, I found a nail file and clippers, a tiny tin of what smelled like licorice Altoids, and a single coin. I swirled its raised surface as if reading Braille.

I considered pocketing the money, but zippered everything back where I found it, set the purse aside and picked up a shoe. The buttery leather felt expensive, probably Italian: Prada, Cavalli, or Gucci. Holding it in my hand I learned Lydia had little and narrow feet. I felt as if I was nestling a finch. An odd feeling of regret washed over me.

There's nothing worse than wasting time. It always landed me in trouble. I made a mental catalog of all the lists I could make if I had paper and pen. Such as itemizing fabrics I hoped to buy, and what I envisioned making from them. Despite the limited light I could have sketched clothes designs. Maybe I'd write a long overdue letter to my friend Amy in Florida. Or start the journal I never had time for, but knew would change my life. Write Roger a filthy love letter, and slip it into one of Lydia's jacket pockets above me. How long would it take her to find it? There was an outside chance I'd pick something she never wore, and finally gave to Goodwill.

How much time had passed? I touched my left wrist and remembered I'd left my cheap Timex on the pricey granite countertop near their stove. Good thing there was no place I needed to be, no one to worry if I arrived home late.

My rear end was getting sore sitting on jagged edges. I gave serious thought to opening the door and walking into their bedroom. I'd been tucked away in the closet long enough. Sliding the door open to a two-inch gap gave me a fuller view of his meaty back. He'd been tighter when we began our affair. His weight on top of me had shifted lately from comfortable to heavy. If I stood, the angle might allow me to see over him to Lydia. Did she look pretty in sleep, or had her mouth fallen open and spittle collected? He released a series of wheezes that sounded like attempts to whistle. I smiled, thinking about the sleep of the innocent.

I felt behind me to the closet's back wall. Underneath a canvas satchel I found a hard plastic case, eight by ten, with a handle. I lifted it around to my lap. Heavy, like a drill. But why hide a drill? When I pushed the knob to the side, the latch clicked open loudly. One of the two in bed snorted but didn't move. I slipped the cold, hard object out of its niche. Not until I molded my hand around it did I realize it was a gun.

The hair on my arms rose. The weapon was hidden on Lydia's side of the closet Did she know Roger cheated on her? Maybe she'd planned to wait until he fell asleep, creep to the closet, grab the gun, and shoot him through the heart. She'd watch his blood puddle around a gaping hole, trickle to the side, and soil their dark-chocolate paisley matelasse bedspread. She had enough money to replace it. I'd attend his funeral incognito and grieve inconspicuously.

I aimed the barrel toward his end of the closet. I'd never handled a gun, but assuming it loaded, I faced the barrel away from me. My face felt hot. I began to sweat. It's odd enough holding a gun, but holding a gun while naked is another thing altogether.

My thoughts cleared the longer I held the weapon. If the woman opened the closet door, I'd shoot her in the groin. But why go to prison? Maybe I'd burst out of the closet naked, Roger's semen drying on my thighs. Confront her. But about what? I was the one in the wrong.

I set the gun in one of her spike-heeled pumps, barrel toward the toes. Sliding the closet door open an inch more, I saw a stack of DVDs on the nightstand. I strained to read the labels: *300, Saw II, Police Academy III.* No doubt his idea of good movies.

If I closed one eye I saw a narrow cross-section of their bodies. Leaning forward gave me a wider view: his back, left arm and leg draped over her. I positioned the gun barrel in the door crack and aimed for the base of Roger's skull. A prickle of heat shot up my spine. When he snorted, I dropped the gun, but caught it mid-air. My hands shook. Again I directed the barrel, gauging the likelihood of a bullet passing through his neck bones to enter her skull.

I put the gun back inside her shoe, and took several deep breaths. The musk of sex mixed with dust filled my nostrils. Someone sat up in bed and inhaled sharply. Bedspring creaks followed by a thud to the floor that I felt in my bottom. I leaned to see Roger's feet—two toenails discolored and misshapen by a fungal infection. I usually suggested he keep his socks on during sex, saying his feet were cold.

"What time is it?" Roger said.

"What?" Lydia's voice slurred from sleep.

"Come on. I want a big fat burger, and a mess of greasy fries."

Petite feet with nails painted poppy-red, probably manicured at Sableaux Salon. It hurt to see her painfully thin ankles. Did she worry about never being thin enough? How could she walk in those spiked heels? Did she believe they added definition to her calves? I never appreciated how Roger mocked Lydia's impractical high heels, how she walked like a puppet in them. But who was I to defend his wife?

"My clothes are all wrinkled," she said.

"You're fine. Let's go to Spoody's." He sounded way too jubilant and smug. As if he had already gotten away without her discovering his infidelity.

The woman's feet moved closer. "I'm going to change."

"No!" His ugly feet moved between Lydia and me. "Come on, you look fine. We want to beat the happy hour crowd."

She wore a slender silver ankle chain with an embossed heart the size of my baby fingernail. It rested against her ankle bone beside a pale vein. I closed my eyes until they left. Wondering what attracted Lydia to Roger, and what kept her interested.

After I heard his car pull away from the curb, I climbed out of the closet and wandered through her clothes. Impeccable fabrics: hammered satin, alpaca, silk jacquard, brocade wool, charmeuse, crepe. Top designers: Vera Wang, Versace, Armani, Calvin Klein, Ralph Lauren, Marc Jacob, Vanderbilt. I imagined Lydia's tilting voice sounding their names.

I tried on a Blumarine African print dress of chocolate and cream jersey, an Escada caramel lambskin leather blazer, and a Valentino red and white flowered chiffon wrap-dress. Would I be happier owning them?

What made Lydia happy? Surely not Roger.

Would she wear the clothes I designed? I could see her in my criss-cross halter dress of ice blue taffeta. Or my violet and white jersey geometric print dress that buttoned down the front.

The crisp, scratchy linen of one of Lydia's blazers reminded me of Roger's coarse hair. The way it felt roughing me up. I could almost hear its divine friction against my fine curls. I pulled on Lydia's Herrera blood-red cashmere sweater. Its plunging neckline showed off my cleavage. In her closet I hung the T-shirt I'd appliquéd from pieces of a damaged antique postage stamp quilt. It hadn't turned out as I'd hoped.

Kneeling in the center of their bed, I wiped the Egyptian cotton sheets, probably 1200 thread count, between my legs. Oh so soft. Sheets Roger never allowed me to slip between. I made the bed nice and neat and smoothed my palm along the exquisite matelasse. Between their pillows, I arranged the gun wrapped in my underwear.

A feeling of lightness filled me. Perhaps Lydia would be as happy to rid herself of Roger as I was.

To the Man on Crutches Lumbering through Sand Dunes to the Atlantic

My friend and I saw you park, wrestle out of the driver's seat, grab the pair of crutches from the back. We watched from our car across the street in the Welcome Center parking lot as we ate lunch on the last day of our January vacation at Kill Devil Hills, North Carolina. The sun through the windshield felt so good on the coldest day so far, only forty-three degrees, with wind that blasted right through to your bones.

It hurt to see you hobble through that soft sand. Your right leg was in a cast from the knee down. I remember how hard it was to use crutches when I broke my ankle, tibia, and fibula five years ago—the same knee-high cast I wasn't allowed to let touch the ground.

I didn't believe you should be driving. I wasn't allowed to for four months, told not to put pressure of any sort on it for two months. Were you accelerating and braking with your left foot?

You sat in your car a long time before you exited. Were you trying to build up your courage? Writing a note to leave on the passenger seat, trying your best to find the right words to explain without blaming?

You weren't dressed for the weather, a short-sleeve T-shirt and shorts. We wore three layers of clothes to keep warm.

You moved in such desperation, I said to my friend. I couldn't imagine what your hurry was, and how you were willing to risk a fall, unless you intended to walk into the sea, let yourself drown.

The water temperature alone would no doubt cause hypothermia. A few hours earlier, we visited the aquarium where they'd rescued twenty large sea turtles washed up on the beach because the water froze them.

Several times you slipped and almost fell as you climbed through the narrow opening between dunes, sand too soft to get any traction.

We couldn't see your license plates, but maybe you were on vacation like us, only just arrived, and couldn't wait a minute longer to see the ocean. So, you stopped at the first beach you reached.

Before you arrived, we'd visited the same small beach, part of Cape Hatteras National Seashore. It's deserted and wild. *You're wearing flip-flops. Watch out for the seabeach amaranth—fleshy leaves that vine up through the sand in every direction.* Its red stems gave me the creeps. The beach is littered with black, leathery egg cases of skates, a fish related to stingrays and sharks. They have pointy-looking tendrils on each end. Someone told us they're called *devil's purse.* They freaked me out, reminded me of the giant Hercules scarab beetles from South America that I saw at the Cincinnati Zoo. Their oversized set of horns horrified me.

Three crows, the same inky, iridescent black, flipped over the egg cases, jabbed their beaks at the more penetrable underside—a crunch that, combined with their raucous caws and an overpowering gamy smell, made me gag.

There were also several large jellyfish, clear blobs that jiggle, but they've no doubt dried out and died by now, so I don't think they can sting you anymore. But I couldn't imagine they'd be pleasant to step on, and could cause you to slide, lose your footing. I knew only too well how hard it is to get up from the ground with crutches, when you can only use one leg.

Don't trip over that denuded, gnarled loblolly pine half-buried in the sand at the crest of the dune.

My friend said I was letting my imagination run away with me, but I was sure you were going to come to a bad end.

We finished our lunch. Needed to return to our condo to finish packing. We'd leave for home early the next day. Fifteen minutes had passed. You hadn't returned to your car. I wondered if we should call 911, but what would we report? If you'd walked into the ocean, you'd already be dead.

As we drove away, I mulled over possible reasons. Did your wife leave you? Did you lose your job? Were you homeless? Had you fallen into another bout of bottomless depression? Was this your first attempt to kill yourself?

I never learned what happened to you.

I hope you stood and stared at the endless blue, the horizon barely distinguishable, water mirroring sky, waves' soothing roll and slither, tiny piper plovers that hop and peck. As you stumbled toward the ocean, the sun caught a seven-inch lightning whelk shell tumbling near you—biggest you've ever seen. You couldn't resist leaning to pick it up. It was perfect. Ginger-brown stripes radiated down the sides from the spire to the bottom, pearly white on the inside whorl. You tucked a handkerchief around it, slid the tapered end carefully in your back pocket. Thought how happy your daughter would be when you lay the spiral in her palm.

Living Without

It was a night for musing. I sat with my long-distance friend Riza on the porch of her cabin overlooking the Licking River, swollen from late spring rains. In the country, darkness is different than in the city, the air thicker and softer. When you lean back and collect a mouthful, it tastes sweet and rich as the musk of spring soil. Neither of us had spoken for several minutes. In the country, you use fewer words, but you say more.

We sat in side-by-side canvas director chairs with a narrow rectangular table between us. I felt the heat of her forearm when I reached for my glass of wine. Seven votive candles in cut-glass holders flickered on the porch railing. We could not see the river, but I sensed its current underneath our words. I thought about how the Licking flowed north, same as the Nile. Across the water, a neighbor's cows released sounds like someone calling a loved one.

From the side, Riza's face looked oddly flat, as if all its planes aligned perfectly. She lifted her glass to her lips and closed her eyes while the Shiraz entered her mouth. Before sipping mine, I inhaled the earthy aroma that hinted mushrooms, violets, and berries—its fragrance exquisite as its taste. The wind carried whiffs of the sandalwood candles.

I only saw Riza four or five times a year. A hundred miles divided us. We met in a tai chi class seven years ago, when she lived in the city. We felt comfortable with each other from the very beginning. Joked that we were twins separated at birth, though she's a tall blonde and I'm short and brunette. We were born a year and five days apart, close to the spring equinox. Riza's 40, I'm 39. After tai chi classes, I could have sworn she was flirting with me.

She took my hand, her thumb coming to rest on the ticklish skin near my wrist bone. "Mia, I've met someone."

Her honey-colored hair glowed in the candlelight. A silk paisley scarf clasped her long waves in a ponytail high on her head. Loose wisps framed her long, thin face. Curls burrowed in the nape of her neck. Her scarf matched her gypsy outfit—a long full skirt and top of thin silk that revealed every curve. The large paisley pattern contained deep purple, turquoise, and orange. I was still obsessed with black and white or dark chocolate and white clothes in flower prints or geometric designs. She claimed it related to my fascination with black and white photography.

"I know I said I was done with men." Riza had a knack for finding the kind she wanted—men who climbed mountains, excavated shipwrecks, led African safaris. Inevitably they left, minutes before she threw them out. She said his name was Bray, that he raced motorcycles.

As I set my glass down, my elbow grazed hers. I lingered, pretending to steady my glass. Her skin felt warm as a fieldstone hoarding sun.

With an inheritance from her mother she'd paid cash for her cabin on eighty acres. Area farmers leased outlying fields to raise tobacco, soybeans, and corn. She sold handmade three-dimensional art compilations she called "nestings," which incorporated whatever she found in nature— dried flowers, grasses, leaves, feathers, wasp nests, twigs, bones, animal fur. I suspected she wove her cat's hair into her creations. A shop in New Jersey couldn't keep her work in stock, pestered her to make them faster. But you couldn't rush Riza into anything.

"Where did you meet him?" I asked.

"Hooters." She'd made the mistake of allowing her brother to pick the restaurant to celebrate his birthday.

"Your new man likes Hooters and he was attracted to you?"

She swatted the air near my face. I caught a whiff of mint soap from her skin. She cupped her small breasts in her palms. "He likes my nub-bins."

Her throaty laugh pulsed through me. Earlier that morning, we'd skin-ny-dipped in the river, one of our rituals. Her areolas were the most beau-tiful shade of rose.

The best part about her new man, Riza said, was that he lived in Clarksville, Tennessee, and traveled from track to track, so he wouldn't be in her hair all the time. She shifted in her chair, as if snuggling against him.

"Do you have anything in common?" I asked.

"We both like to be naked."

Her voice slowed as she settled into the luxury of describing him. The candlelight flickered shadows across her face. She unknotted the silk scarf from around her ponytail, gathered and smoothed all the loose strands, retied the scarf. I wanted to undo her hair and bury my face in its thick waves. I kept my thin, fine hair short and body-permed; otherwise it stuck to my head like a skullcap.

"What's got into you?" I asked. "What happened to the girl who told me intelligence was the strongest aphrodisiac?"

"She got lonely. Now she's getting fucked silly."

"Enough said."

"Bray's skin has a peculiar smell." She scrunched up her narrow, straight nose. Her eyes were deep-set and spaced far apart. "It's not offen-sive, but it is odd." She reached to pet Rattatat, curled on her bare feet. The cat's fur resembled a spotted leopard. One of the spots on her back looked like a fiddle.

I said it sounded like a personal problem. She explained that his skin retained the odor even right after he showered, kind of metallic, antiseptic, and Rattatat always wanted to lick him, which Bray didn't appreciate. At the mention of his name, the cat leaped onto Riza's lap.

"Hey, you've had some weird boyfriends yourself," she said.

"Oh, yes. Mark—Mr. Diddly."

He played with himself while watching TV, reading, driving a car. Even when we had sex, he was always reaching down to touch himself.

As she stroked the cat, her arm came close to mine and then retreated, in rhythmic waves of warmth.

"Men are so self-involved, it's pathetic," she said.

"Which says something about us, I'm sure."

"Maybe we should switch to women."

I pushed her shoulder, laughing as if her suggestion was the most outlandish thing I'd ever heard. My voice echoed across the water. Bullfrogs answered. Riza picked up the empty bottle of Shiraz, and headed inside for more. She mentioned cutting up some cheese and making popcorn. I volunteered to help, but she insisted I stay put.

The family of flying squirrels stirred in the eaves above me. Rattatat's back arched. Earlier one of them had fallen into a chair, belly up, but managed to lunge out of the cat's reach. The scent of the cabin's wood stove mixed with the rich mud of the river after a downpour and the sweet heaviness of spring. Between bullfrogs and tree frogs, if you really listened, you heard the river. On the other side, the cows shifted positions and released forlorn moos that traveled on the water.

The day's events washed over me. We'd completed our tai chi routine along the riverbank as the sun rose. Spent the day catching up as we walked through woods, fields, and along the riverbank. Riza returned a beached mudpuppy to the water. We picked dandelion greens, chickweed, and purslane for a salad and collected gifts the river left behind: bones, mussel shells, driftwood, and a snakeskin. With my new digital camera I collected pictures of flowering redbud and dogwood, bur oak and a massive Kentucky coffee tree. She gathered fallen branches for the tree cemetery in her side yard, where buried branches rose from the ground like charred skeletons.

When we skinny-dipped in the river, I looked like an albino beside her deeply tanned and freckled skin. Our nude swimming made me more than a little uncomfortable, because I had to edit where my eyes fell and for how long. On one hand I loved the abandon of it and on the other hand I felt hyper-nervous. Especially this time, because I'd vowed to tell Riza I was bisexual before the weekend ended.

I snapped a picture of her on the pretext of capturing a gnarled sycamore behind her. Turning her body in profile, she lifted her arms and arched her back in a long stretch, her lips puckered in a pouty kiss. She continued to change poses. I snatched each one. Hanging from the limb of a tree, her breasts arced upward. Her back to me, standing among tall cattails, her palms at rest on the fuzzy spikes.

"Get one of me rising from the river." She flounced into the water. "Like Aphrodite."

She slid under and remained motionless for several seconds. The surface had almost healed over when she broke through with a surge. Eyes closed, rivulets rolled down her. When she raised her lids, her look of want and delight stunned me. I was the one who'd lowered my gaze.

From the kitchen came the sound of Riza cursing as she rummaged through what sounded like pots and pans. Quiet followed. I heard my own breath. It mirrored the whisper of wind ruffling tender spring aspen leaves—hearts with serrated edges. Since the cabin was built on a hill, the porch was set high up. On the ground, near the support beams, something snorted. The candlelight did not extend far enough to see. It made no further sound, as if it was listening as intensely for me as I listened for it. Hairs rose on my arms when I envisioned a black bear hoisting itself over the porch railing. I scrambled inside to join Riza on the opposite side of the kitchen island.

"What happened?" Riza asked.

"I heard something."

She laughed. I told her I almost felt the force of air through the creature's nostrils, something much larger than me.

"Might have been Bigfoot." Riza winked. She wore no makeup except for a thin line of emerald under her lower lids, which emphasized the clear green of her eyes.

Intoxicating aromas wafted down from dried lavender, sage, and basil swags hung from the ceiling above us. On a nearby shelf, a branch of bleached driftwood held an empty bird nest in its crook. Tiers of feathers strung together served as kitchen curtains.

I made the standard joke about men with big feet, and watched her cut the remaining cheese into bitesize cubes, fascinated, as always, by how she worked with knives. The knock of the blade punctuated the staccato of the popcorn uncorking its fragrance in the microwave. Her fingers were delicate. A hammered-silver ring I'd made, of two snakes braided together, encircled her index finger.

"Seriously, have you thought about having a gun out here?" I asked.

"You know I'm too impulsive to have serious weapons around."

We made several trips to get our feast outside. I followed Riza, enjoying the way her ponytail swished side to side like a pendulum sweeping her neck, pointing to the fineness of her shoulders.

She swept a heavy-duty spotlight across the field in front of us, illuminating a deer at the riverbank. "There's your Bigfoot," she said. "No doubt munching more of my tulips. Thinks I planted them just for him."

Settling back in our chairs, we each cradled a bowl of popcorn in our laps. The cheese tray lay on the table between us. I asked Riza to tell me more about her new man. As we talked, we dipped cheese nuggets and pieces of popcorn in our wine.

"He has golden skin and hair spiked out in a Rod Stewart look. And he makes me feel golden."

The pleasure in her voice settled on my skin. I looked across the river, above the treeline, to the stars and crescent moon still on the rise. A patch of fog moistened my face and with it came the scent of a wood fire. We'd seen the neighbor across the river burning dead brush.

"Mia, you have to go places to meet someone, you know."

"I take classes. Did I tell you about the amber beads I ordered from Russia?"

"I don't think you'll meet any men in your jewelry-making classes."

For years I've collected beads, and attended classes to learn styles and techniques of jewelry making. Filled notebooks with designs, but only completed a few pieces.

"Mia, do you want to adjust claims all your life? When are you going to finally quit that damn job and start a jewelry business?"

"I guess when I'm ready to be poor."

She said you learned to live a simpler life. If you needed a new roof, you just patched it and set out bowls to catch leaks. She fixed only what she absolutely had to. "You'd be surprised what you can live without."

I wondered if she referred to our love lives. Her voice had fallen. The words "live without" barely reached my ears.

She raised her wine glass in my direction. "Here's to new ventures." Her words sounded forced.

"And when can I meet your new venture?" She seldom introduced me to her men.

Her tender-green eyes flattened. She looked toward the river. Undid and refastened her ponytail. It swayed before coming to rest at the nape of her neck. "He's married."

I said I was sorry and leaned to touch her shoulder. The tip of her ponytail tickled my thumb, sending ripples of pleasure up my arm.

"There's nothing to be sorry about." She flung a fistful of popcorn on the porch floorboards. Rattatat pounced, playing with them before lapping them up. "All I was looking for was a little sex, a little fun. He fits the bill quite nicely."

"A little is all you get when they belong to someone else."

"Belong is such an ugly word."

"But it's a truth you need to keep in sight." My voice reflected the bile rising in my throat. "It takes an incredible amount of energy. You think you're up for it, you think he's worth it, but it begins to undermine every part of your being."

My words hung in the air. I wished I could snatch them back.

Riza eked out a laugh. "What are you talking about?"

"I did what you're doing." I told her how, two months ago, I'd broken off a three-year affair with a married man.

"Did it end badly?" she asked.

"No. Quite civilized. Good fucking to the very end, but all discreet and contained. No mention of love or any kind of emotion really."

I replayed how once, while making love, he forgot himself and accidentally said he loved me. He pretended he never said it, and so did I. The awkward moment passed. We continued the affair, but that was the beginning of the end. He'd gone too far, and was afraid what might happen next.

"What an asshole," she said.

"He wasn't what you'd call generous of heart. Had a streak of stinginess that ran clear through. Eventually I told him I'd met someone else."

"You let him off?"

"Why not?"

She looked into my eyes before asking if I'd have married him if he'd divorced. I answered no, but my voice revealed my uncertainty. Riza pried no further, but questions shadowed her eyes. I breathed deeply and concentrated on the freckles sprinkled across the tops of both her cheeks and the bridge of her nose like flecks of cinnamon.

Turning back to the river, she tightened her ponytail, and asked if I'd seen him again.

Every Tuesday and Thursday at tai chi, I said. The S.O.B. started flirting with another woman in class. Thought he was being subtle.

"Men are never subtle," Riza said.

"It made me so mad that he didn't have the decency to find a new lover somewhere else. But more than that, it pissed me off that it bothered me."

"You know what you should have done?" She filled her mouth with popcorn, and added a sip of wine. "You should have said you had an STD. Or you found a girlfriend that satisfied you like he never could."

I laughed. She joined with her throaty version. I wanted to touch her neck.

"Would you ever get involved with a married man again?"

The bullfrog's bellow matched the ache in the pit of me.

"I don't really believe in it. But it was something I needed to risk once." My voice cracked.

"I wish I could say the same." She forced a laugh that couldn't hide the underlying sadness. All her men were married.

We fell silent. I closed my eyes, and listened to the trees. When the rustling died down, I heard the river. More a feeling than a sound as water coursed past.

"I'm afraid to have a man of my own," she said. "It's safer to enjoy them a fuck at a time. I never have to worry about it failing, because it's doomed from the start."

"Don't you want more?" I hadn't expected my voice to shrill with such longing.

She looked away from me, toward her tree cemetery. Said she liked her solitude for the most part. Wasn't ready to give it up yet. What man could match the companionship of Rattatat and the trees and the fields and the river? She raised her arms as if to hold it all. "Besides, I'm easily bored. I don't keep men long enough to grow tired of them. And I don't have the stamina. They take too much out of me."

I wanted to tell her she deserved more happiness than she could contain.

The tree frogs' chorus rose to a crescendo, ended, and began another ascent. A mist hovered above the river.

"Riza, I'm envious as hell of you. You do whatever the fuck you please. I'm afraid I'll never quit work, never start a jewelry business."

She picked up her chair and placed it directly in front of mine. Our knees touched. Goosebumps rose on my arms as I lifted my eyes to hers. Her wide, thin lips mirrored the lines of her pale eyebrows.

"You need to give yourself a deadline," she said. "Quit work in the fall. You can live here rent free until you get things going."

I asked what I would do with my apartment, my furniture. She said why not rent it as a furnished apartment. If there was anything really valuable, store it in her shed.

"Are you serious?" I asked.

A wind gust creaked strips of loose bark on the aged locust arching over the porch.

"I'm offering you a place to stay for a year." She smoothed her hand down the silk scarf that had blown around to the front. "After that, we'll see."

I took several deep breaths, dangerously close to tears. Could this actually work?

Riza's cabin contained two bedrooms, a roomy kitchen/dining area, and large family/living room. She'd converted an outbuilding into a two room studio. I pictured us working on our different art in connected rooms. Taking walks, gardening, sharing meals.

Riza suggested I submit my photos to magazines to generate some income. "They're unusual," she said. "You take them from weird angles, and use interesting filters and backgrounds."

I'd framed her one of my photos she particularly liked—taken from beneath a basket of airy asparagus fern hanging on a shepherd's hook. The sun to the left rendered the needles translucent. In the background, clouds crammed the sky.

I leaned to lift my glass, and the porch planks squeaked.

"More secrets?" Riza asked.

I gulped the remainder of my wine, waited for the spreading warmth, and inhaled the green opening-up of spring.

Riza's mouth formed a wicked smile.

Heat flushed through me. "I knew it. You've known all along, you little shit."

I grabbed her hands. She didn't resist. A pale blush spread over her face and neck. What more would she allow?

"Now that the cat's out of the bag, so to speak." She looked directly into my eyes. "What's it like to make love to a woman?"

"Let me show you."

She pulled her hands away and scooted back in her chair. "Let's get this perfectly clear. You get the guest room. I'm not sharing my bed with you."

"One can only hope."

She crossed her arms over her breasts. Not before I saw her raised nipples. Candlelight sputtered behind her head like an aura. Over her left shoulder, beneath the span of stars, I could barely see the outline of the hill that led to the road out. The cows' lament echoed across the water.

Much of her hair had worked out of the ponytail. She undid it, releasing golden waves.

"Here, can I put it up?" I asked.

She narrowed her eyes at me. I moved behind her and gathered the swirls in both hands. The soft strands spilled between my fingers, and I leaned into her mint musk.

Morphing

Sylvia points to the iguana, camouflaged in the lush canopy high above them in Krohn Conservatory. "See him?"

Jared glances for a second before turning away. He works as an associate professor in the Zoology Department of Miami University. On summer break he has grown his light brown hair longer. It hangs in clumps. She wonders when he has last washed it. His black jeans and T-shirt look and smell as if he has retrieved them from the dirty clothes hamper. He is a meticulous dresser when not depressed. But in the past three months he has burrowed further and further within himself.

"There," she says. "See his tail curled along that huge palm leaf touching the ceiling?"

"I don't see it," he says. He doesn't try to disguise his disinterest.

She resists the urge to say, "You would have seen it a year ago." When they'd visited Krohn's Butterfly Exhibit on their third date, he spoon-fed her fascinating facts while ten thousand butterflies from all over the world fluttered around them.

Sylvia had not told him about her fear of flying insects and birds, but panic pulsed in her when wings hovered near, at Krohn's. She snapped photo after photo of question marks, paper kites, and swallow-tails perched on salvia, ageratum, and verbena—unable to deny the butterflies' beauty.

A Krohn employee had dispersed sugar-water onto fingertips that day. Children balanced butterflies on extended index fingers. Nearby a father told his daughter to be careful, that its wings were already tattered. The girl's blue eyes widened and her bottom lip quivered. Sylvia wanted to wrap her arms around the girl. How satisfying it must feel to show your child something new, she thought. She could imagine Jared teaching a son or daughter about ferns, mosses, conifers, and how delighted they would be when he imitated sounds of seals, camels, jaguars.

He had taken her hand and explained that butterflies couldn't repair their wings. When it rained, they hid under overhangs of houses, leaves, rocks, or in bushes with their heads down and wings held tightly together. He pressed her hand between his palms.

In a sea of Stargazer lilies a birdbath had contained butterflies with a six-inch wingspan of mottled brown. Jared said they were Blue Morphos that lived in Peru's rainforests. Their undersides allowed them to blend with their surroundings. The large eyespots along the edge of their wings scared away predators. Immobile as if drugged by the sweet treat, the Morphos feasted on the juice of browning orange slices.

"They drink juices of rotting fruits through their proboscis." He had spoken close to her ear. "They uncoil their long, flexible tongue to drink, and when they're done, they roll it up again into a spiral." He flicked the tip of his tongue in the swirl of her ear. Her inner thighs tensed.

Several Blue Morphos had fluttered their wings and alighted. She sucked in her breath when they neared. She couldn't believe how deep-blue their wings looked inside, when they flew.

He explained about the thin layers of hardened protein called chitin which colored the wings by reflecting and refracting light through thousands of overlapping scales that acted as a prism. A Morpho landed on her forearm. With its wings closed, she could only see the furry brown with the surreal eyespots. She whisper-screamed for Jared to get it off her—heart racing, face warming.

Behind her, he had rested his hands on her shoulders. The wings flut-tered open, only for a second, to reveal their inner blue. The butterfly tick-led her skin like rose petals. She held her breath.

"The scent hairs of the males smell like vanilla when pinched." His breath had flamed the nape of her neck.

She had fought the urge to shake the Morpho off her arm.

"They use scent glands to attract mates." His words had flowed thick and slow as honey. "During sex, the male and female remain connected by their abdomens for fifteen minutes to as long as three hours."

His words had warmed her ear. "The Incas believed butterflies ap-peared at sacred places like Macchu Picchu. We'll go there someday."

He had layered detail upon detail, talking her through, until her heart slowed. He said American Indians believed if you whispered a wish to a butterfly it came true. With his spearmint gum he wet his index finger and lowered it toward the butterfly. It climbed on. Slowly he raised it near his lips, mouthed something, and released a feather-breath to blow it away.

"What did you wish for?"

His eyes had moved over her body. "I'll let you know when it comes true."

As they walked through the conservatory, she had become more and more intoxicated with Jared and his knowledge, with the colors, shapes, and patterns of the butterflies and flowers surrounding them. He pointed out how the Lacewing's orange matched the ruffles of the Queen Sophia marigold. The liquid green of the Banded Peacock mirrored the leaves of the Margarita sweet potato vine. The wings of the Paper Kite gleamed with the same transparency as the Angel Trumpets. A glass atrium contained an endangered species, Queen Alexandra Birdwing, showing its life stag-es from egg to larva to chrysalis to adult, when it reached a wingspan of twelve inches.

Jared had read the exhibit notes aloud: "When the butterfly breaks out of the chrysalis, it hangs upside down, its wings wet and limp. It pumps blood into the veins of its wings, expanding them all the way out, then they dry and," he raised his eyebrows, "harden up."

He'd looked into her eyes. "There is nothing like the first time it flies."

To commemorate that day at the Butterfly Show, he'd given her a butterfly necklace of tiny amethysts in a gold filigree setting. She'd worn it on this one-year anniversary of the first time they made love. He hadn't noticed, though several times she'd brushed a fingertip along its wings as if to release magic dust.

The glass dome of the palm house ceiling arches forty-five feet tall, glutted with palms, ferns; a rubber tree reaches the ceiling and starts back down to meet its base. Jared used to enjoy holding her hand, but now he hurries ahead of her. She doesn't understand how he walks past all the beauty without a glance. Just entering the conservatory, walking between the exquisite stained-glass panels, has opened and expanded her heart and lungs. She loves being among all the growth. For years she has dreamed of earning a horticultural degree, but the time or her financial situation never seems right. She doesn't dislike her job in accounts payable at a construction company, but she can't say she likes it either. Isn't it time to do something she loves?

Problems with Jared had begun after their first two months together. Subtle changes that didn't add up to anything in themselves. He fell asleep in movie theaters. If she stayed weekends, he slept a good deal of the time, saying he was worried about not having enough publications and how it would affect his hopes of tenure. Things irritated him—the way she interspersed "uh-huh" in conversation, how she sometimes snorted when laughing, and her habit of curling the ends of her hair around her fingers.

Maybe her touch would reawaken him. He used to love her hands on him. She catches up and smooths her palm in the hollow between his shoulder blades. He pulls away. She takes a deep breath of the oxygen-rich air, telling herself not to take it personally. But how else can she interpret it?

She follows him through the tunnel beneath the waterfall. The cool air refreshes her flushed face but reminds her of the time they'd walked through it before, when he'd moved her against the wall and kissed her.

She remembers the cool stones pressing against her back and the heat of his lips.

They stand side by side on the bridge facing the twenty-foot falls. The railing's round post, smoothed by seventy years of hands, reveals rings of the tree it came from. Translucent water turns opaque as it tumbles against the limestone, suffused with green from nearby maidenhair ferns, betel nut palms, and corkscrew palmettos. His fingers look so thin, the skin slack. He's lost more weight, rarely eats anything healthy. She's tried to introduce some vegetables, fruits, and beans into his diet, but he prefers meals of red meat and potatoes, most often fried.

Three and a half months into their relationship, Jared had begun canceling dates and showing up an hour or more late with no explanation. If asked why, he turned sullen and belligerent. He flared up at some supposed tone of her voice, or something he claimed she insinuated about him. If she suggested they make reservations for dinner before a Saturday night play at the Aronoff Center, he accused her of being too rigid. Just go with the flow, they'd find somewhere to eat, he'd say. Hadn't he told her early on that he refused to live by the clock in his personal life, since his life as a professor forced him to follow a timetable?

Sylvia edges her hand closer to Jared's on the rail until she feels his heat. He does not respond. She closes her eyes. The cool mist from the water's motion settles over her, soothing her skin.

A year ago, he had taken her hand at the same waterfall and asked her to close her eyes. He'd whispered, "A year or two, and we'll hear the roar of Iguazu Falls, tango in Argentina, see giant tortoises on Galapagos Islands, and party at Carnival in Rio."

She had ingested the essence of water, soil and chlorophyll, the scents of growth, along with his musk.

"We'll glide down the Amazon, hike the rainforest." He'd infused her with the names of animals they'd see. "Marmoset, armadillo, anaconda, coatimundi, capybara, kinkajous, ocelot, piranha, tapir." He imitated calls of macaws, cries of spider monkeys, and roars of jaguars.

He used to carry on conversations in the voice of Al Pacino, Ralph Fiennes, or Viggo Mortensen. Now, he rarely imitated, as if he'd already pulled his last trick out of the bag. But every so often the intriguing, kind man with an irresistible sense of humor emerged like tulip tips from the cold, hard ground.

When she opened her condo door an hour ago, she had experienced an all too familiar apprehension over which version of Jared would show up—the sweet, sexy man or the cold, cynical one. Each time she made up her mind to end the relationship, they would have a glorious weekend hiking at Land Between the Lakes, exploring at Mammoth Cave, or whitewater rafting at The New River. Then he wouldn't call for a week at a time, and if she called him, he made it obvious he wasn't in a mood to carry on a phone conversation.

Now she holds tight to the bridge railing and chances a peek at him. Lately his face has been so devoid of expression, it has pained her to look at him. His eyes are closed. Is he also remembering their third date, wondering how to spiral back to the beginning? Maybe everything is all right, after all. They've just hit a rocky spot.

A daddy longlegs crawls on the stones bordering the waterfall. Sylvia remembers the time they camped overnight on the Appalachian Trail near Asheville. In the morning they had discovered a clump of what looked like a hundred longlegs interlaced, clinging onto a tree trunk near their tent. He had calmed her down by stringing her odd bits of information about them: how their legs contained thousands of sense organs yet were so fine they couldn't penetrate water, how they molted by unzipping their body case and dragging their long legs out of their old skin, how their legs were made up of seven segments and a very flexible foot with a curved claw.

She touches his hand and points. "Remember the camping trip where we found that ball of daddy longlegs?"

She concentrates on the rush of water and imagines its clarity and magic draping them like a safety net. "Mmm. I wish I could have this at my house."

"You can," he says. "Run some bath water."

She turns away, not letting him see her tears pool.

"I was kidding." He forces a laugh and moves around her to the tropical room.

She follows, taking her time, sounding the plant's names softly, cocooning herself in the tapestry of root, trunk, branch, and leaf. Bougainvillea vines hang at eye level with leaves shaped like elongated hearts. Tentacles of strangler figs form masses of knots, loops, braids, and circles round the trunk and branches of a Madagascar palm. Curved thorns grow along a vine called Cat's Claw. The label says it grows in Amazonian rainforests. She thinks of the file cabinet in her study glutted with travel brochures they ordered about The Azores, Zanzibar, Mozambique, Belize, Spitsbergen, Borneo and Ecuador. She has never yet ventured beyond the United States. They talked about so many vacations in the beginning of their relationship. Sylvia believed they'd happen.

Through a film of ferns, she sees Jared push past a clog of people. A tangle of multiple trunks rise to a dense umbrella-shaped canopy of thick leaves. "Dragon's Blood," she reads. "Named for the reddish resin its bark and leaves secrete." On their visit a year ago, he told her the tree possessed magical powers because, according to legend, it sprang from the blood of a dragon slain by Hercules. He knows so many stories, so many interesting details about insects, plants, and their interdependencies. Many tales have ended with promises to take her to their exotic homeland.

If only he'd consult a doctor about his depression. Seeing him walk stooped over ahead of her, she wonders if she has ever met the real Jared. If you strip away all his jokes, impressions, and catalogs of information, who is this man she fell in love with?

He blocks her way out of the tropical room. "Where do you want to eat?"

She doesn't answer. They have only been inside the conservatory for a half hour. The orchid display, the desert garden, and the bonsai room remain to be visited. Beside a Passion Flower, an iguana squats. Its muscular green tail, longer than its torso, swings slowly back and forth as if poised for attack. Its scales pulse as if with poison.

"Ugh." Behind them a little girl gags. "There's one." She has pigtails the color of pearls, the same as Sylvia had during early childhood. Her own hair turned dark blonde as an adult. She lightened it until she turned thirty, when she cut it short and let the real color grow out.

She nudges Jared. "Isn't she cute?"

He rolls his eyes and walks away. Jared doesn't want children. She agreed with him when the discussion first came up after several months of exclusive dating. But uncertainty has seeded within her, sprouting roots everywhere.

She inhales the fragrance of Rangoon Creeper and brushes her palm against the thick tangle of Spanish moss. Its softness surprises her. As she draws her hand away she spots a five-inch-long walking-stick insect, at eye level. She hurries away, thinking about the time Jared took her into the Cincinnati Zoo's insect house. Despite her fear of spiders and other insects, she'd agreed to enter. As terrifying as they were, there had been something fascinating about a foot-long centipede, a ten-inch praying mantis, and hundreds of three-inch long hissing cockroaches. Only because they were behind glass.

Sylvia catches up with Jared and reaches toward his hand, but she pulls back. He has made it more than obvious that he does not want to be touched today. An iguana skitters in front of him, and its claws scratch the cement. It dives between two patches of Persian Shield—purple leaves with livid-green veins. Jared's stride never changes, as if iguanas dart past his feet every day.

The little blonde girl is behind them again. "Where did it go?" she squeals.

The girl's excitement nudges Sylvia into wondering if she would ever experience having a child. Her first marriage ended in divorce after twelve years. At thirty-five, she is running out of time.

She leans over the lantana to see the tip of the iguana's tail alongside the serrated edge of blood-red coleus. The woman and child move past.

Jared releases a dramatic sigh of impatience.

"What's going on?" Sylvia asks. "You act as if you don't want to be here."

"I don't happen to like this place as much as you do."

"You act as if you don't want to be with me." The heat of the room intensifies her volume.

"I'm just not in the mood today," he says.

Sylvia wants to claw his eyes out. "In the mood?" Her voice echoes. "You mean to say you have to be in a certain mood to be with me?"

"No." He raises his hands shoulder level, as if to keep her at a distance. "I mean I'm having an off day."

"More like an off month, or two or three."

"It's totally unrealistic to expect me to be happy and affectionate all the time," he says.

"Maybe, but I expect you to at least not act like I'm a noose around your neck."

He walks away from her into the desert garden. Next to the Devil's Backbone, she grabs his arm.

"We're not going to fight right here in front of everybody, are we?" he asks.

They are the only people in the desert garden.

"Yes, we are. Let's get it over with, once and for all."

He turns away and points to two butterflies resting on a pencil cactus. "Look, they're fucking."

"Humor isn't going to get you out of it this time," she says.

"Out of what?"

Their voices spike beside the Crown of Thorns. An iguana claws its way across the tile floor ahead of them, its tail thumping.

"What is going on?" she asks again.

He edges away from her until he backs against a contorted euphorbia with crested branches snaking in every direction.

"Either you make a doctor's appointment this week, or I'm done. Your depression is getting worse. There has to be something they can give you, something that won't interfere with you getting tenure." She spits the last words.

Lately everything hinges on whether he will or won't be granted tenure. If he can get a full professorship, surely everything will be all right. But how long should she be expected to wait?

"What do you want?" She digs her words into him, trying to break through.

"Do you think I want to be like this? Don't you think I want to be happy with you like we were before? I can't help this. I can't turn it off and on."

Sylvia has read extensively about depression to understand what he is going through. She has tried to get him to join a gym with her, take salsa dance lessons, or take up kayaking.

She moves close to his face. "Then do something about it."

"I don't like drugs. I don't want to walk through life like a zombie."

"My god, what do you think you are now? You've never even tried any medicine. Will you see a doctor, just once, just for me?"

"I don't think it will help. I've had these black moods all my life."

He has never told her this. She'd assumed the depression was a recent development.

"These are not moods, Jared. You're clinically depressed."

She hates the sharpness of her tone. He looks at her as if he's seen her for the first time. His eyes dart away.

"What are you so afraid of?" she asks.

He tries to brush past her. She cuts him off.

"Do you want to continue like this?" Her voice surges in the hot air. "What do you want?"

He doesn't answer. He stares at the floor.

"I know what I want." Her body feels swollen with heat, her skin tight enough to crack. "I want a man who at least knows whether he wants to be with me or not."

He flinches when she touches his arm.

She says, "I'm fucking tired of feeling as if I'm walking on eggshells."

Sylvia sees the movement of an iguana climbing toward the glass dome. An area of the ceiling has been opened to let the thirty-foot flower stalk of the Century plant bloom through. She's read that it only blooms once, after twenty to fifty years, dying afterwards. It smells like rotting meat.

Jared's face remains empty. She is overwhelmed by a desire to dig her fingernails into his cheeks. "Get out of my sight."

He releases a sound like air escaping a tire. His shoulders lower, and his body softens. He hurries for the exit as if running for his life.

Sylvia doesn't budge. Legs rooted, she takes a deep breath and steeps herself in the heat and glut of growth around her. An array of haworthia graces the sand; she notes the plant's size ranges from a quarter to a dinner plate. Its compact rosettes of leaves are plumped with water and dotted with white spots, evenly spaced. She bends to see what is speared on one of the rosette's points—crisp coils of something translucent. Three feet away, an iguana, dragging itself between a Blue Candle and an Old Man cactus, has dislodged patches of cracked skin on the cactus needles. She heads for the flowering jade at the end of the desert room and the entrance to the orchids.

Blueprints

Tina and her husband Dale stopped at a Marathon station for gas and a snack. Dale chose a cashew log, Tina a bag of Frito Lay corn chips which left an oily film on her lips and in her mouth. She wanted to rinse with mouthwash, but it was packed away in the trunk. As they munched in the front seat, Dale grew quiet. Tina wondered if it was just his typical anxiety over plans and their execution. He'd mapped out their entire vacation like one of his blueprints. They hadn't traveled for the past four years because of his architecture firm's massive downtown rehab project. It would have satisfied her to fill a suitcase and head west. Stop whenever they grew tired for the night. All they needed was a bed, a toilet and shower, no bugs. He insisted on booking reservations for each nightly stop, which required them to keep to the precise schedule he'd worked out. They were eating snacks to forego lunch, because they'd hit construction that he hadn't factored into his itinerary.

After they finished their snacks, Tina went inside the shop to refill her Diet Pepsi. When she returned to the car, Dale had the map of Tennessee and Arkansas spread out on the seat. His frown told her they must be seriously behind schedule.

In the upper corner was a small map of all the states, on which he had their course plotted. They were making a box of the country: beginning at Greensboro, North Carolina, going west across the southern states, until they hit California, traveling north up the Pacific Coast to Washington, returning east across the northern states until they reached the Atlantic Coast, and south to home. Every stop they made, he marked the time in deep purple gel-ink next to the round or diamond-shaped city. He loved maps, just another form of blueprint. Working for the past fifteen years as a legal secretary in an all-male law firm, she'd had her fill of following men's timetables.

She wanted to smooth away the grid of lines on his forehead. He was a worrier—his latest concern whether they'd be able to afford their dream home. Tina knew what her mother would have said about it. Tina could hear the barbed, self-righteous tone that had been aimed at her more than once. As a therapist advised Tina, she envisioned the memory of her mother, along with its negative energy, consumed by flames. Tina took a deep breath, and as she released it, imagined blowing away the ashes. Stay in the present, she told herself, concentrating on her husband's face lowered toward the map.

How many lines had she etched into his face over the past ten years of their marriage, and how many more would form before their dream home was completed? Tina had learned in a stress handling workshop that building a new home was right up there with divorce and death of a spouse. She hadn't believed it then.

The high humidity made Dale's dark brown hair form loose curls. She smiled, remembering when he'd worn it long. He'd finally given up his long hair when he turned thirty—five years ago. She'd been sorry to see it go, but couldn't deny it was thinning. Tina loved it when he gathered it into a thick ponytail, and waves fell onto his forehead. She touched the ridge of his left eyebrow where the clear mole caused a gap. His bristly hairs tickled. He looked up, and his eyes shifted from amber-brown to golden-green.

She ran her index finger along a dog-eared fold of the crinkly map, until she touched the tip of his baby finger. He responded with a smile that warmed her from scalp to toes. She wanted to draw his hand to her lips, the curve of her neck, her breasts. But she held back, savoring the ascent of desire. Like a tight bud, she luxuriated in anticipation of letting loose later.

Dale slowly refolded the map into a neat rectangle. He believed in taking care of one's possessions. After cutting their lawn, he took the time, no matter how exhausted, to rinse off the grass clippings and dry the blades. At the end of each autumn he emptied the fuel and changed the oil.

She always felt safe with Dale. Looking at his hands, with their nails neatly clipped, she remembered how on their wedding night, her father told Dale he'd better take good care of her. Chills had run up her spine. When she was thirteen, her father seduced a neighbor woman half his age. When her pregnancy began showing, word spread quickly. Tina hadn't understood the source of her parents' escalating fights, until a boy on their street asked her how she thought she'd like having a bastard sister.

Tina took a deep breath, and chided herself for dredging up those memories.

"Ready?" He prepared to turn the key in the ignition.

She asked if they could delay a few moments longer, while she completed seated stretches before embarking on the last leg of the first day's journey. He surprised her by acquiescing. From a storage compartment alongside the console he removed a thin leather portfolio, and slid out a series of blueprints. She couldn't believe he'd brought them along, but smiled, acknowledging the fact that he could not sit without doing something.

She had no idea constructing their dream house could be so complicated. Three separate schemas—one architectural, one electrical, and one for the plumbing. Each required its own legend with unique symbols similar to a highway map.

How different Dale and she were. Whereas she found the schematics marginally interesting, he actually enjoyed studying them, same as she liked reading a book about the history of color, or watching a documentary on Leonardo da Vinci. At college, she'd started out as an art major, but switched to art history, because she liked studying others' art more than creating her own. She'd dreamed of working as an art museum director or curator, a gallery owner or exhibits designer, an art auctioneer or appraiser. Those jobs were scarce and highly competitive. After graduation, a relative told her of an available job at a law firm. She took it, telling herself it was only temporary. Now she merely collected art. But she often thought about taking an art class once their life settled.

Dale balanced the diagram on the dashboard before he removed his wire-framed glasses. He cleaned them with a pre-moistened cloth (individually wrapped) in a zippered pocket of his overhead visor. The blueprints reminded her of a school textbook with images of the human anatomy. Each transparent overlay diagrammed one of the body's systems. She'd found the skeletal, cardiovascular, and digestive systems most disturbing. But the sound of the inner parts entranced her: ligaments, phalanges, clavicle, and duodenum, jejunum, ileum. And the way each half of the body mirrored the other. How the pieces coupled and purred by impulses. She thought of da Vinci's "Vitruvian Man." All the intricate correlations of human proportions.

Worry lines returned to his face. He turned sideways in his seat. "Honey, there's something I need to tell you." Honey. She loved hearing the word on his tongue.

Tina thrust herself across the cloth seat away from her husband. He leaned toward her, face clenched, eyes soft-sad. When she snatched her purse from the shaded hollow near her feet, her elbow overturned the twenty-four ounce Styrofoam cup full of Diet Pepsi and ice. The liquid cold engulfed her left foot as she swung open the passenger door into the August heat. She slammed the door, not looking back, cutting short his voice calling her name. Why did he have to tell her this, now, on the first day of their month-long vacation? Why hadn't he waited until they were home? Did he expect her to suck it up, and continue with him across the United States after he confessed to infidelity and fathering a child?

She hurried toward the women's restroom, a dirt-colored concrete-block structure detached from the store. Her soda-soaked foot made a sucking sound in the leather gym shoes. Her head swirled with symbols—the dots and dashes of state boundaries they'd cross, and shots of Dale entwined with another woman, cradling an infant. The radiance of his face seared her.

Ten feet away a man hosed off the blacktop. The tarry smell rose in steam that made her think about the hot springs they planned to visit as they traveled through the upper part of Arkansas. They had picked out a deluxe Jacuzzi for the second level deck of their dream home, outside the French doors of their primary bedroom. Planned to close in the sides of the deck with a privacy fence, and leave the front open to the woods. The deck was angled in such a way that it was doubtful anyone would see them. They hoped to use the Jacuzzi year round, in the buff. On their fifth wedding anniversary they'd flown to Desert Shadows Inn, a nudist resort in Palm Springs. Even though she knew she'd never see any of the people at that resort again, she'd prided herself on taking a giant step in self-acceptance. But what good did that do her now?

Her head pounded and her stomach churned. All their plans to visit The Grand Canyon, mountains, beaches, deserts, rainforests, museums, art galleries, theaters, monuments. She couldn't believe her mind kept returning to their vacation. She'd longed to see Oregon's Crater Lake, its two thousand feet high cliffs, formed by the collapse of a mountain seven thousand years ago after a volcanic eruption. How she'd like to slip beneath the lake's deep pure blue waters.

The rancid smell of gas burned her eyes and the inner membranes of her nose. She almost collided with a woman in tight jean-shorts and a glaring-yellow and black striped tank top. The woman released an indignant huff. Tina envisioned squashing her like a fat bumblebee.

A young, pregnant woman carrying a toddler came out of the restroom smoking a cigarette. Tina wanted to shake her and jerk the cigarette from between her lips. No, she'd really like to slap her hard. It scared and exhilarated Tina how close she came to doing it.

The restroom doorknob felt like a hot coal. She slipped inside the room not much bigger than a side-by-side refrigerator box. The heavy metal door slammed, reverberating in the soles of her feet. A wave of sickening-sweet deodorizer mixed with the stink of a dirty diaper enveloped her. On the wall above the toilet, a sign with bold black letters warned, "Ladies, please do not flush fenimine items." The misspelling fueled her rage with the assumption that plumbing problems were caused by women flushing tampons—another example of men's ignorance when it came to women.

She wound sheets of toilet tissue around her hand layer upon layer like wound gauze. When she exhausted the first roll, she tore the cardboard off the holder, and a full roll fell into place with a satisfying click. She glanced at her wristwatch: 4:30 p.m. She unrolled the paper as fast as she could. Any minute now, Dale would be at the door. They were due in Memphis at 10:00 p.m. The next evening they planned to spend at Magic Springs and Crystal Falls in Arkansas. He had it mapped out so that they could visit seven theme parks. They shared a love of roller coasters—the higher, the faster, the more jerks the better. They'd met at Paramount's Kings Island, working summers while attending college in Cincinnati. The names of roller coasters they planned to ride raced through her mind: Boulderdash at Lake Compounce in Connecticut, El Toro in Jackson, New Jersey's Six Flags, and Hydra at Dorney Park in Pennsylvania.

"Tina?" Her husband's voice sounded different, changed into someone else that quickly. Or had he slowly mutated all these years until he reached the point where he spewed his confession? She wondered how long his affair had lasted, and if this was his first. He'd never have told her if the woman hadn't gotten pregnant. Had she, he, or both of them purposely gone without protection during sex? Maybe the woman wanted to trap him into marrying her. The neighbor her father impregnated chose to give the child up for adoption. Tina's mother stayed in the marriage. They moved from Tennessee to Ohio, where an uncle got her father a job at Ford Motors. What choice did her mother have with a teenage daughter to raise? Tina's mother had never worked outside her home. Tina vowed never to allow herself to get into a position where she could become trapped.

She removed the toilet paper from her hand, and threw it on top of the other wads in the toilet bowl. How naive she'd been to think the same thing that happened to her mother couldn't possibly happen to her. To believe she could protect herself from hurt.

Dale tried the door. Honey, please let me in."

In answer, swinging the toe of her gym shoe into the rounded side of an aluminum garbage can, she gouged shapes like wide smiles. The garbage can tumbled over, spilling a dirty diaper onto the concrete, releasing its stench. Her stomach turned, reminding her of the time she thought she was pregnant during their third year of marriage. Not wanting to trust her hopes to home pregnancy tests, she'd waited thirty-eight days before making a doctor's appointment. She couldn't believe it when Dr. Hess told her she had not conceived. Her breasts were tender. She felt nauseated in the mornings. Her periods never came late. The doctor explained hysterical pregnancy, suggesting they take a long vacation—relax and forget about wanting to have children—suggesting that sometimes stress caused temporary impotence.

Dale had refused to reveal the woman's name. Actually asked Tina what difference it made. She asked why he was protecting the woman, because if he intended to be a part of his child's life, wouldn't the child also be part of her life, as his wife? If she was ever able to conceive, this other child would be her child's half-sister.

Tina's family had loaded up a U-Haul truck, and left their rented home in the middle of the night like criminals. She'd never told her friends goodbye. The letters she later wrote them were never mailed. A blanket of shame settled over her.

When Tina had asked how involved Dale intended to be with the child, he didn't have an answer. Dammit, he said, I just learned about this myself; I don't know how it will work out. But he insisted on keeping the woman's anonymity intact. That was the point at which Tina had bailed out of the car.

With each kick to the garbage can, Tina told herself she would not disappear like her mother. If Tina chose to stay in her marriage, she'd fight to find a way through the pain to the other side. Her toes had begun to ache, but she continued to dent the can. Such pleasure, this acting out. Thrum of muscle and bone, leg and abdomen—pouring everything into the motion of destruction. She had never been a violent person. Couldn't even stand to kill spiders that happened into their house. She swathed them in a tissue, carried them outside, unwrapped and released them.

Each kick she delivered with perfect precision like a clearly enunciated word. Maybe if she punted enough words, she could unlatch the door between them.

Her ribs throbbed. She stopped to catch her breath. An engine started, followed by the sound of tires pulling away. Dale would never leave her. He was the most dependable man she knew.

She leaned her ear against the door. Heard ragged breathing. Hers or his? She closed her eyes to listen. Nothing.

Who was the other woman? Had Tina met her at the firm's Christmas party?

Tina tried to visualize the female architects and office associates her husband had introduced. But no, the woman and Dale probably agreed she better not attend the party, lest they give themselves away. An odd term, she thought—give themselves away—yet how appropriate. Dale had given himself away to another woman. Just like that. As if his relationship to his wife meant nothing.

"I'm sorry, Tina." His voice sounded so far away on the other side of the metal door. She believed he was sorry, that he hadn't meant to hurt her, that she was the one he loved—all the clichés rehashed on TV soap operas, sitcoms, and movies. Now it was their turn—Dale, Tina, and the other woman in their own tired triangle. She could picture them in the endless parade of losers on the Jerry Springer Show.

"Won't you please—"

She screamed with everything she had left in her, as long as her breath lasted, and punctuated it with another kick to the garbage can, this time with the heel of her shoe. Blood rushed to her face and throat, the same sensation as when her husband pushed inside her. She screamed again, feeling the veins of her neck stretch as she opened her mouth wide. Tina had no idea she could scream so loud, or that one simple admission from her husband could release such violence. Her voice echoed off the walls, wrapped around her with the vigor of a long awaited embrace.

"Tina?"

The plea in his voice tore at her. She backed away from the door. When the sink nudged her spine, she turned and screamed into the mirror. She stared at herself—splotched face, eyes fiery brown, red hair wet with sweat—as if observing a stranger. Questions flooded her: whether the people in his firm knew about his infidelity, her infertility, and the other woman's conception. No, she wasn't going there—worrying about what other people thought. What happened with her own marriage was between her and Dale. Not the other woman. She and Dale could decide. Options reeled through her mind. Divorce. But she couldn't say she was through with him.

She wrapped paper towels around her fist and shattered the mirror. Slivers stung her forearms. She didn't check for blood. The adrenalin rush echoed the drug of impending sex. The sex she'd anticipated all fucking day, as she passed through city after city, over river after river, unaware of the secret coiled inside her husband.

Splintered glass glittered in the black sink like fallen stars. Who in the hell bought a black sink for a restroom like this, she wondered? Then she remembered that Dale had chosen one for their retro black-and-white bathroom. Tina envisioned hanging her small black-and-white art on the wall across from the commode. She collected tiny paintings and enjoyed arranging them in ever-evolving collages. Recently they'd attended even more local art exhibits, seeking treasures for their new home.

"I'll make it right."

She barely heard him, but it was so preposterous a promise, she almost asked him how.

He had told her he did not love the woman; he had no intention of marrying her, but he guessed he was obligated to support the child. He'd tried to convince the woman to get an abortion, but she balked, saying she didn't believe in murder. Tina kept thinking that somehow she and Dale would work everything out, because she was not running away from their dirty little secret like her parents tried to do.

She clasped her hands around the liquid soap dispenser attached to the wall, pulled with all her strength. Something ripped inside her as the dispenser came loose. She slung it against the metal door behind which her husband waited. Cream-colored soap splattered her thighs like semen.

Another voice joined her husband's. An argument.

"I said I'd pay for damages."

Yes, let him pay, she thought. Someone should pay. Who better than him?

"Give her a break. She just found out a drunk driver killed her sixteen-year-old niece."

How convincingly he lies, Tina fumed. How long had he been lying to her? Yet, if she had been asked to describe her husband in one word, it would have been "honest."

"What if she hurts herself?" the other man asked.

"Then we'll call a fucking ambulance. Don't you have a key?"

"She's got it bolted from inside. Mister, don't even think about suing me if your wife hurts herself on my property."

Someone wrenched the door handle. "Tina, the owner's calling the police."

Feet firmly planted on concrete, she grabbed hold of the toilet seat.

Why care about germs anymore? Let all the piss and shit of the world enter her. Hadn't it already? She pulled hard toward her gut, grunting with the effort. It wouldn't budge. With part of the broken soap dispenser she dug at the clips that held the toilet seat in place, clawing like a person buried alive.

One set of footsteps walked away. The other continued pacing parallel to the door. Dale no doubt wondering how he'd get out of this tight spot. She thought of the 3-D puzzles he liked to work on. One called "Rush Hour" with cards for various beginning configurations of a crowded city parking lot. You had to get the red car out of the only exit, by moving the other cars up, down, left, right. For his thirty-fifth birthday last year, she'd bought him another one called "City Puzzle, The Builders Challenge." A metal grid of buildings you arranged into one city block. He'd designed at least ten similar puzzles he hoped to market one day.

Heat radiated from her shoulders, biceps, triceps. Sweat stung her eyes. She stuck her head under the faucet, wet her hair and face. From the dispenser she yanked one paper towel after another, and patted the dripping. When she turned the water off, she no longer heard Dale's footfalls. The possibility of abandonment vibrated through her.

She resumed her attack on the toilet seat clips. Her wedding rings dug into her finger. When she tried to remove them, they would not budge past her knuckles.

"Hey, honey. Remember that bistro at Penn Yan?" Dale's voice wavered between laughter and tears. "That piano man, remember, he sang with a terrible falsetto, 'The Lion Sleeps Tonight?'"

For their first anniversary they'd traveled to New York's Finger Lakes, where they hiked woodlands, through gorges with waterfalls, toured vineyards and salt mines, sailed for an entire day on Lake Cayuga. Talked about one day building a vacation home there, later buying a sailboat, eventually retiring and opening an art gallery. Afterwards, they'd almost been ejected from their bed and breakfast when they drank a bit too much wine. She remembered him twiddling his fingers at her, leering. Declaring it was mandatory, for any man who stayed at Finger Lakes, to perform certain duties. They'd dubbed the place Fingers Lake.

Outside the door, Dale hummed a few bars. The lion sleeps tonight.

Her stomach started to shake. He always hooked her with humor, reeled her in without a struggle. Not today. She dug at the toilet clips.

How hard it had been not to laugh. To pretend the male singer sounded divine. Their table was arranged at an angle so they both had full view of him at the large white piano. He looked like a blonde Elvis during his sequined jumpsuit days.

Would she tell her coworkers, or keep it secret? All the divorce papers to fill out and file. Documents of their failure. It would take years to erase Dale's name from everything, sort themselves out from each other, and start over. So many of their friends had divorced, some more than once. Their bitterness wore her out.

At least there would be no child custody battles, no wrangling over visitation rights. He'd never impregnated her. Dale had wanted to adopt. Tina balked, citing horror stories of adoptions in the news lately. She turned paranoid, imagined preordained reasons she'd not conceived— some sort of punishment or test. Remnants of her abandoned Catholic faith. Maybe she had very little time left to live. Or the end of the world neared. Sometimes she wondered if she could turn herself around to think that she was blessed by being childless. It left her unencumbered, so that she could immerse herself in art.

Her nasal passages unclogged. Her sweet-sour sweat cloyed with the diaper mash and maraschino deodorizer gagged her. Dale resumed pacing.

She'd wanted to see an infertility specialist, get to the bottom of the problem, find a solution. It surprised her that Dale didn't want to. She suspected he feared he'd be proven inadequate, defective. Instead it was her. It infuriated her that his infidelity didn't bother her as much as his fathering a child. It pointed the blame squarely on her shoulders. And it was the kind of mistake that would never go away. Like an ever-expanding foundation crack—spidering longer and wider each year.

When one of the toilet hinges finally gave way, the other fell apart with one jerk. Tina slung the toilet seat against the metal door. Shatters exploded in every direction, stinging her calves. One of the larger chunks landed in front of the door. An index card taped to it read, "Please leave this restroom in the same order as you found it."

She picked up a triangular chunk of porcelain and flung it at a narrow window above her. Glass tinkled onto the concrete like delicate chimes.

"Honey, please open the door. I just want to see if you're okay."

His voice, familiar as her breaths, in and out. Soles scuffed the pavement, back and forth in front of the door. He had always been a pacer. She remembered how happy he looked that morning. Tying the laces of the Timberland boots she'd bought him for the trip. He'd wanted a pair for years, but couldn't justify their price. She never understood why he demanded so little for himself.

Tina needed to sit a minute and rest. She'd sweated through her clothes. Her arms were so tired, she could barely lift them. She leaned against the sink, and listened to her panting breaths. The closing scene in "One Flew over the Cuckoo's Nest" flashed before her, where the tall Indian ripped a sink from the wall, or maybe it was a water fountain, and smashed it through a window to escape. She hoisted herself onto the sink and bounced. When she heard a crack, she dismounted. Elbows resting on the cool porcelain, she pushed down with all her weight until the sink separated from the wall. Water spurted everywhere.

She surveyed the scene of her crime one last time. Satisfied her anger had consumed itself for now.

Her husband's pacing had stopped. Underneath the door a thin stream of sun glowed. A cricket crept toward her, its body onyx in the liquid light.

To hell with luck, she thought. She and Dale would decide what they wanted. Tina flushed the toilet and watched water rise over the rim before she unlatched the door. She slung it open, almost knocking her husband down. She had only enough strength left to crush the cricket, and walk to the car. She'd let Dale clean up the mess.

Cornerstone

The couple was a hundred miles from home, on the Daniel Boone Parkway, nearing Hazard, Kentucky for Briar's thirtieth high school reunion. They'd left a few days early, to enjoy the October countryside, the trees at their height of fall color. At Laurel River Lake they canoed. In Gray Hawk they attended a Bluegrass festival. After the reunion, they planned to hike part of the Appalachian Trail to Buzzard Rock in Virginia. Over the past ten years they'd backpacked a few sections each year, tracking their progress on a map hung in their study. There was nothing like the sense of connection, of being at home in your body, in your marriage, in the world, that resulted from walking the woods in silence. Climbing over giant rock formations, wondering where they originated, and what forces brought them to their present location. Gwen found it easiest to breathe in forests. Trees sweetened the air.

Briar pointed to her right. Just inside the first line of trees, two deer nibbled underneath a shagbark hickory whose leaves matched the goldenrod swags on the roadside. The forest appeared on fire from so many shades of red, yellow, and orange foliage.

"Good eyes," she said.

He smiled, and tipped his hat toward her.

"You and that hat." She loved him in the floppy golf hat, though it could hardly be described as anything but nerdy. It covered his thinning hair, but he claimed he wore it to protect his pale skin from the sun. He'd already had two cancerous lesions removed, one from his arm and the other from the crown of his head. Quite a scare. The doctor warned them initially that the cancer might have spread into his bone or blood.

Gwen felt herself tearing up. She turned too late toward the passenger window.

"What's wrong?" he asked.

She leaned to kiss his cheek. "I'm just happy. I wish we could take a month-long vacation."

But that wasn't happening any time soon. He'd worked late at his computer software company for the past two months, in order to take these few days off. He'd been on twenty-four hour call the past ten years. Had grown thinner than ever, and rarely slept through the night. Wasn't breathing properly, but remained tepid about the breathing exercises she suggested.

How was she ever going to tell her husband that for the past two years she'd been having an affair with a woman? Gwen thought it would peter out in a month at most. She feared he'd consider it a deficiency in himself, that he couldn't please her. But that wasn't true. She didn't understand why, but her sexual desire for him had elevated. Maybe because someone new found her attractive. Could it be that simple?

As selfish and convenient as it sounded, Gwen didn't want to hurt Briar. My God, what a cliché. How many times had she seen tawdry movies in which the man, caught in an affair, swore he loved his wife, never wanted to hurt her?

Why did this have to happen? She'd never had an affair before, never even been tempted. It was so unfair to Briar.

She filled her lungs with air, held for a count of fifteen, released to a count of ten, envisioning oxygen-enriched blood bathing her organs. He smiled at her, no doubt thinking *there my wife goes again with her whacky breathing exercises*. Five years ago, she had rented office space and begun a practice as a transformational breath facilitator. She analyzed clients' breathing patterns, and devised exercises to more fully engage their respiratory systems, oxygenating their entire bodies, nourishing them down to the cellular level.

Speaking the names of towns they passed, (Goose Rock, Hima, Yerkes, Bluehole, Spurlock, Thousandsticks), she wondered what it would be like to live in a small, rural community. Would there be a need for a breath facilitator in Hazel Patch, Biddle, or Pongo?

She unlatched her seat belt and scooted closer to massage Briar's neck and shoulders. He released a deep hum. They'd long ago left the range of their favorite alternative radio station, WNKU, and had forgotten to pack any extra CDs. They could listen to Norah Jones, Eric Clapton, and Ray Charles only so long, before resorting to whatever local stations they picked up, mostly what Briar dubbed hard-boiled country.

He flinched when she pinched the area halfway between his neck and shoulder. No, don't stop, he said, dig in there. Gwen thought about how she needed him relaxed. Again she imagined the words she might use to tell him. She might make light of her secret by saying, think of the fun they could enjoy together, from their newfound common bond, the fact that she now saw women in precisely the same way he did. He'd look puzzled, but intrigued, and she'd go on to explain that something had shifted within her. She found women as beautiful as men did. She'd pause to let those words sink in, before adding, "I'm having an affair with one, in fact."

Ridiculous to imagine she could joke about the situation. How was she ever going to tell him? Anticipation intertwined with dread, made it hard for her to fully expand her lungs, leaving her stuck in a hypersensitive state somewhere between arousal and hysteria.

They wove in and out of the Appalachian Mountains. Veins of coal lined rock faces. Beds of leaves filled the culverts, plastered the pavement. It had rained earlier in the day. Now the sun flashed through gaps between trees to create a psychedelic effect at the edge of her vision, making her queasy.

Briar's cell phone rang. She grabbed it from the console between them.

"Is that Shelley?" he asked. "She left a message at work. I never did get back to her."

Gwen closed the phone when she heard only a dial tone. "Must have been a wrong number."

He searched her face momentarily before turning back to the road. Could he tell how keyed up she was?

It was dusk when they turned onto Route 15. She saw so many abandoned farmhouses in various states of collapse. How sad, she thought, trying to picture how they once looked. Briar slowed and pulled off onto a gravel path, to get out and stretch his legs. She crossed the road to a set of six stone steps rising to a flattened field that had no doubt once held a house; a few crumbling stones all that remained of the foundation. She stood where she gauged the house's center to be, raised her hands palm up, as if to receive blessings. Six water maples, three feet in diameter, formed a circle of shade around her. She stood in their vortex, breathing in their musk, feeling the energy, the warmth of lives that had once filled the space, so happy she could hardly contain the surge. With the euphoria came the realization that her entire life might come tumbling down around her.

Gwen carried a larger fragment of one of the foundation stones to their car, picturing where she might place it in their backyard perennial garden. Briar helped make room in the trunk for her find, wrapping it in an old quilt they used for picnics. As they continued to travel, she pictured the foundation stone riding in the trunk, between their suitcases.

It was dark, and Route 15 had few lights. It looked as if they were riding into a black hole. The hair on her arms rose. Briar looked her way, brow bunched. The car's air seemed to congeal. For a time, there was no sound but the engine's hum and the whir of tires. She snuggled the leopard-spotted afghan around her shoulders, and took several cleansing breaths.

No matter how many times she thought about it, she couldn't conceive of a feasible way to ease into telling her husband she was having an affair. Maybe she could ask him to clear his mind of everything, and think about what was important to him. Ask him to let go of everything he'd learned or heard about relationships and love. To think about what she meant to him. No, that was too manipulative, not fair at all.

Pockets of fog drifted toward their car. She'd begun to feel as if they'd slipped into a time warp in one of the hollows, a space they might never find their way out of.

Once inside their hotel room, Briar pulled her onto the bed, gave her a long kiss. "Let's get a bath together. Did you see the size of that tub?"

Her eyes pooled with held-back tears. "Let's take a walk first. Get some wine in that liquor store we passed." Over the years, she'd noticed how walking, keeping your body in motion, helped when discussing difficult subjects.

The streets of Hazard were deserted. It felt as if the entire world held its breath. Briar's pace gradually slowed, hers quickened, until they matched. He took her hand.

The roots of massive maples, oaks, and elms raised the sidewalks, poking through in gnarled humps like scars, or secrets that refused to stay hidden. Gwen had begun a scrapbook of trees encountered on their hikes and country rides through Kentucky. Sycamores were her favorite, but she loved so many trees: mimosa, sassafras, buckeye, catalpa. Earlier that morning, in a town called Burr, she found a locust tree with leaves glittering golden like the fringe of a rare tapestry.

As they passed under street lights, she stepped over a perfectly symmetrical imprint of a small scarlet maple leaf. She wondered what forces, what processes had broken down the soft leaf, bleeding it onto the sidewalk. Had she melded into her twenty-two year marriage, into Briar? Could she separate herself any longer?

She thought about the miscarriage she'd suffered in their second year of marriage. It had felt as if her entrails, her entire being, had ripped out of her. She never conceived again. Doctors said she and Briar had a genetic incompatibility. Maybe they should have adopted a child.

Gwen felt as ancient and constricted as the trees they passed. She took a couple of prolonged breaths and began.

"I love you, and I'm happy, happier than I've ever been." She tried to slow her words, calm the emotion welling up in her. If she started crying, she'd never finish.

"I used to think," she said, "that people could get all their happiness from each other, but I'm not sure that's true."

My God, she thought, this wasn't at all what she planned to say.

"Gwen, what the hell are you talking about?"

She kept her eyes fastened on the sturdy oak heaving the sidewalk thirty feet ahead. When they passed it, she'd pick another tree to mark her progress—a practice she developed early in life to steady herself and lead her forward. She could use any large object, but trees worked best.

"I met a woman." Her face flushed. She felt like a small child made to feel dirty and guilty. "Something crazy happened to me. I still don't understand it."

They walked a few steps before she said, "I'm having an affair with a woman."

Briar stiffened, pulled his hand from hers. "How did this happen?"

She said she didn't know. She didn't go searching for a female lover, or any lover for that matter, but she met a woman in her chanting group, and they had a lot in common, became friends, grew closer, and started thinking of her sexually, which freaked her out and excited her at the same time.

She couldn't slow down. Her breaths came in spurts, her words like a levee let loose. Her throat felt raw.

"I need a fucking drink," Briar said.

She followed him across the street to the liquor store. He grabbed two bottles of bourbon from the display stand near the counter. One under each arm, he hurried to their hotel room, not bothering to check if she followed. He walked slightly stooped over, away from her, as if protecting his face from a cold wind. They passed a sapling, bare of leaves, under the hotel parking lot light. She shivered, turning away from the sharp shadows of its branches.

Inside their room, they sat at a small table by the sliding glass door to the balcony. He poured them each a plastic cupful of bourbon, his face ashen. They swallowed large gulps. It scared her the way he clenched his jaw, as if he'd already decided something, and wouldn't be swayed.

"I never wanted to hurt you." Her voice cracked. "I don't know what got into me, but I became obsessed with the idea of making love to her."

She hadn't planned to tell him such details, but she couldn't stop herself from explaining how she asked the woman one evening, over a glass of wine, if she'd ever been with a woman. She'd said, no, but she'd wanted to try it. Next thing Gwen knew, she found herself telling the woman she was beautiful, sexy, intriguing, and that she wanted to be with her.

She didn't know exactly when her perception of women shifted, when she began noticing women's bodies in an altered manner: the way fabric stretched across their breasts, or how a low-hanging crystal necklace caused Gwen to imagine sliding a finger down past the vee of the woman's sweater. Instead of merely noting to herself that a woman had beautifully shaped lips, she began to wonder how it would feel to kiss them. Gwen didn't believe she'd ever encounter an opportunity to find out, and just wrote it off as part of her peri-menopausal sexual upswing—a guilty pleasure. But the more she allowed herself to imagine, the more detailed and intense her fantasies grew.

Gwen tried to slow her breathing. Why wouldn't he say anything? She repeated that she didn't want to live with this woman. Their relationship was primarily sexual. She saw her once or twice a month. "Briar, you're the one I want to share my life with."

He guzzled more bourbon, refusing to meet her eyes.

"She knew from the start that I was never leaving you. I know you can't believe me, but this doesn't have to ruin everything between us."

"How could it not?" He slammed his palm on the tabletop. The open bottle tipped, but he snatched it up without jostling out any bourbon.

She forced herself to remain seated, hoping to make him understand what she herself didn't fully comprehend. When she touched his hand, he jerked it away, and looked her full in the face.

"You fuck some dyke for two years, and now you suddenly feel all guilty, and want to confess your sins?"

"You son of a bitch." Gwen grabbed her cup and headed for the bathroom. She filled the tub with water as hot as she could stand it, and emptied a vial of lavender bubble bath beneath the faucet. With the water cradling her, she tried to empty her mind, slow her breaths, still her heart. Tears streamed down her face. Their saltiness reminded her of semen, and she wondered if she'd ever taste Briar again.

She sipped the bourbon and listened for sounds from the other room. All she heard was the barely discernible sound of bubble bath suds popping. Had he fallen asleep? Holding her breath, eyes closed, she slid underwater. At the age of five she discovered how much she loved submersion, gliding along the pool bottom, or just below the surface. Water softened, lightened, and muted everything.

"Gwen!" The water distorted his voice, but not his tone or volume.

She pierced the surface, heart racing, water sheeting down her. Briar moved toward her, arm raised, as if to slap her. He'd never verbally or physically abused her, but maybe all bets were off. But he was only reaching for a towel, which he pulled off the nearby hook and handed to her. She patted her face dry and wrapped it around her hair.

He sat on the closed commode, elbows on knees, shoulders hunched. "Why did you tell me this?"

She finished off her bourbon. "It's your sister's fault."

He sat up straight. "My sister? What in the hell does Shelley have to do with this? You're not fucking her too?"

Gwen slapped her palm against the water's surface, wetting his jeans. "You know how I feel about your sister." She clamped her lips together, determined not to retrace old battles. "I need more bourbon."

He refilled her cup, hands shaking. She took a swig, and described the night he was out of town the previous week. Shelley stopped over the house, uninvited, of course, and instead of knocking, walked in and found her and Rae kissing in the kitchen. They were just having a glass of wine before leaving for the theater. Gwen's face burned, remembering the sweet taste of wine on Rae's lips, followed by the shock of seeing Briar's sister in the doorway.

"Shelley had the most evil, pleased look on her face. Probably orgasmed, she was so happy to finally have some dirt on me."

Gwen took another swig of bourbon, closed her eyes, and tried to picture all her resentments against her sister-in-law draining out of her pores into the hot water, diffusing, dissolving.

She told Briar how for a few days she held onto the hope that Shelley wouldn't tell him. But there was no mistaking the look in her eyes. She would tell him eventually, but she wanted to savor the control she had over Gwen.

He held his face in his hands.

"I wanted the chance to tell you myself, to try and explain. I don't want to lose you."

She still believed that the exhilaration and freedom of doing something so unlike her, so far out of her comfort zone, had changed her for the better. She'd carried the new exuberance into her life with him.

Briar left the bathroom without looking at her. She saw him stop at the dresser, shove the room key into his pocket. He eyed the cornerstone she'd asked him to bring inside. He placed his hands around it as if to steady himself. In profile his face looked calm. She called his name seconds before he lifted the stone and flung it toward the carpet. It cracked into several large chunks. She felt the impact. The vibration churned up the tub water. He left their hotel room, slamming the door.

She wanted to go after him, but felt so cold. Grabbing the bottle of bourbon on top of the toilet tank, she chugged it.

She would give Rae up. That was their understanding from the beginning. If either woman wanted out of the relationship, they would be honest, but gentle. They called it their experiment. Neither had made love to a woman before. Gwen remembered the exhilaration, the near hysteria she felt that first time. They'd rented a hotel room with a Jacuzzi. Rae had packed a picnic basket of cheese and wine. They remained clothed while they ate on top of the bed, sitting Indian-style. When they agreed to remove their clothes simultaneously, they laughed wildly when they saw they'd both worn bathing suits beneath. Once they warmed up in the water, they agreed to remove their swimsuits, looking openly at each other, without turning away.

Picturing Rae's auburn curls, the pearl-blush of her breasts, Gwen gave way to sobs. She couldn't stop shaking. She slid under the bathwater, where everything flowed warm and soft. Where she didn't have to worry about breathing.

She felt a thud, as of a doorknob flung against a wall. Gwen came up for air, thinking Briar had returned. Her eyes fell on one of the broken cornerstone's chunks. The ceiling light revealed tiny recesses in the rock's surface and its natural glints.

She was so tired. Again she slid beneath the water's surface, its touch reminding her of Rae's skin.

I've got you," Briar said. "You're okay."

Gwen couldn't stop shaking. Something rough pressed against her, and her skin prickled raw. She must have fallen asleep in the bathtub.

"We've got to get you dried off. My God, have you been in the water all this time?"

He kept coming at her, trying to make her do something, tangling her arms and legs up in something. Her head pounded.

"That's three hours. You'll probably catch pneumonia. With as much as you drank, you could have drowned."

She tried to open her eyes, but the light was too bright. He encased her in blankets, propped her head on the pillow, and held a cup to her lips, urging her to drink. With the first sip of coffee, the events of the evening blossomed like the blow of a sledgehammer to the back of her head. The shivering started again. He removed his robe and slid next to her bare skin, wrapped his arms and legs around her. But she felt his reluctance.

She tried to say she was sorry, but her words slurred. He shushed her, saying, right now she needed to keep warm. His breath bathed her forehead as she cried. He smelled like fall leaves.

Gwen woke to Briar picking up the pieces of the cornerstone. On top of the towel draping the dresser, he fit the cracked edges back together, holding the pieces in place. The foundation stone glinted over his left shoulder. When she sat up in bed, he turned and moved toward her.

What She Could Live With

Two dinosaur eggs, bigger than watermelons, nestled into the forest floor beneath a shagbark hickory. Anita touched Perry's hand, a finger coming to rest on a calloused knuckle. He hadn't seen the eggs yet. She wanted to watch his face when he discovered them.

His pale blue eyes widened, unfolding their wrinkled edges. He emitted an involuntary hum. It was one of the things she found so intriguing about him since they started dating six months ago. The sound never varied, always the same single note. At first Anita feared it was the first stage of some disorder like Tourette's Syndrome. She worried about so many things since her husband Teddy's sudden death two years earlier. After twenty years of a happy marriage, Anita felt as if her body had been turned inside out. All her internal organs hung unprotected. She questioned who she was, who she wanted to be, and all her beliefs, from the most insignificant, such as what thread-count sheets she slept on, to whether she believed in God. Lately, she'd envisioned herself learning to paint.

Anita left the trail. She wanted to touch the eggs.

"Can you believe it?" Her voice echoed in the tall firs. "Dinosaur eggs, right here in Logan, Ohio."

She tried to see through the glossy, translucent orbs. If she lifted one, would it break apart, the babies inside jerking, covered in an amniotic fluid?

"Giant puffballs," he stated. "Calvatia gigantea."

Anita could have smacked him. She didn't care what they really were. Why spoil the magic of their walk through the end-of-September woods? She caught herself from saying that Teddy would have played along. He believed time in the woods could cure most anything. Anita agreed. They'd spent part of every weekend in the woods behind their house. Teddy understood the importance of remaining a child at heart.

Perry pointed at the puffballs with his walking stick like a teacher tapping at a compound equation on a blackboard. Tapping, waiting until he roused students to attention. "One of them can hold as many as seven trillion spores."

Anita knelt and touched the orb with her fingertips. It was firm yet soft, as if lined with microscopic hairs. She remembered Teddy telling her that Indians used mushrooms to pack wounds, because they helped blood clot.

"They're edible." Perry's voice floated above her, softer now, slipping out of lesson mode.

He could be so serious at times. Looked a little like an absentminded professor, with his thick-framed glasses and unruly hair the color of butterscotch candies.

"So are you." She lunged to encircle his legs and pull him to the ground.

They squirmed in crunchy leaves. Anita nuzzled the cotton of his teal T-shirt, near his jeans waistband. The musk of his worn leather belt flooded her nostrils, reminding her of black-brown mud churned up from a lake bottom. Perry was so thin. No love handles to get hold of. She told herself she would not think about how she preferred a sturdier frame. Teddy had descended from stocky German Catholic tree farmers.

The sound Perry made, somewhere between a grunt and scream, fueled her attack. She went for his knee-folds.

"I can't believe how ticklish you are. Teddy never had any ticklish spots." Damn. She'd been trying so hard not to say his name.

"Why are you always comparing me to him?" The edge of Perry's voice surprised her.

"I'm sorry. It's hard to act as if the past twenty years never happened."

"I'm not asking you to." He scooted away from her, against the trunk of a white pine.

"What are you asking?" Her tone sounded harsher than she intended. But they'd been through this before.

"That you enjoy our relationship for what it is, here and now, all by itself, not in comparison to anything that came before."

Anita did not want to be angry with him. She didn't want anything to go wrong on their first weekend away. She crawled through the long, spongy white pine needles to sit beside him. She would not tell Perry that Native American Indians used pine oil in their purifying rituals. She would not reveal its antibacterial, antiviral, insecticidal, soothing and restorative powers—facts she learned from Teddy. She'd hold them close like a feather, a locket of hair, or a piece of bone nestled in a medicine pouch.

"I'm sorry," she said. "Don't be mad."

"I'm not mad," he said. "It's done. I never meant anything hurtful."

She lightly touched his leg, as if testing for heat. "I don't want to spoil anything."

He laughed like a parent dismissing some innocent, misguided notion their child nourished. "Nothing's spoiled. Relax and let whatever happens happen. All I'm saying is don't try to mold us into what you had before."

He smoothed his hand down her leg as if trying to defuse his words, and released one of his low hums. "What would your co-workers think about you rolling around in the woods with a man? At your age."

"I'm only forty-seven. You're the one half a century old."

Eyebrows raised, he looked at her overtop of his glasses, which had slid slightly down his nose, studying, as if trying to decode her. Then his face relaxed into the warmest of smiles, and his blue eyes lapped her. She'd seen similar absorbed looks when he examined something he wanted to build, or something broken he wanted to figure out a way to fix. Like the glass-doored bookshelf he saw through the antique shop window in downtown Cincinnati. She would have taken a digital photo of it. But his eyes moved over the piece, memorizing its details. Three weeks later, he gave her a similar bookshelf he'd made of golden pecan wood.

Anita slid her hand under Perry's T-shirt, up to his ribs. Teddy had thick, dark chest hair she loved to rub her breasts against. She remembered the first time she saw Perry naked. So thin, so little body hair, she'd felt as if she had seduced an adolescent.

Perry pulled her onto his lap. He smelled like woodsmoke from the fire he'd built at the cabin. With the very tips of his fingers he inched over her forehead, eyelids, cheeks, and chin. The slow motion relaxed and aroused at the same time. She never understood how, as a tile layer, his hands remained so smooth. One of his many secrets.

"Remember the first time—"

"Shush." He touched her lips with his fingertips. "Just enjoy."

She took a deep breath, closed her eyes, emptied her mind. Coral, turquoise, and violet swirled behind her lids. Time closed down, crystallized into one perfect moment. A crow cawed far off. She pictured its iridescent blue-black coat. No, she would not think about how Teddy had teased that he'd come back as a crow if he died before her. Wind swished trees, a strip of sun warmed her calves, and the aroma of pine fused with the fruity musk of damp earth.

They sat side by side on the crest of a hill overlooking the valley with its surrounding farms. A chestnut horse grazed at the edge of a stretch of tall grasses. It bobbed its head up in her direction, as if to say "hey." The silver roof of a brick-red barn matched the sheen of two nearby silos. A bank of low-lying gray clouds mutated into mountains in the far distance. Clusters of four-inch thorns protruded from the trunk and some of the branches of the honey locust they sat beneath. She wondered how, with paint, she could convey the mottled bark with its interlocked plates. Around them lay twigs with tiny oval leaves already turned butter-yellow, and brown seedpods twisted into spirals as they dried.

Anita pointed to a pod peeled open. "They say that you can roast those seeds and use them to make coffee."

She deliberately did not say, "Teddy said," though Perry no doubt knew who she meant. She'd told him how much Teddy knew about trees from his ancestors' business. But the word "they" hung in the air like a curse, as if she'd screamed her deceased husband's name. But she hadn't. So the sentence passed. It was the actual naming, then, she thought, that wasn't acceptable. Maybe she could live with that.

She took Perry's hand in hers, touched each fingertip, rolled over his knuckles with the folds of skin like waves expanding out from a pebble dropped in a lake. She followed to where each finger joined his palm, starting a chain reaction of tingles along her inner thighs.

"I love watching you do things with your hands," she said.

"I bet you do."

"I'm not talking sex." She smacked his thigh. "Sometimes I'm interested in things other than sex."

He eyed her overtop of the tortoiseshell frame of his glasses. Released a hum. "So you say."

She remembered the first time she saw him fold freshly laundered towels. As if he had all the time in the world. As if there was nothing as precious, as fragile as the towels he was folding. He made sure all the corners lined up, every edge met, smoothing his palm over the looped cotton like the brow of a lover.

The mindful way he handled tools, tile, and wood translated to everything he did. How he cradled plates, glasses, utensils as he washed them. The attentive way he turned a tomato, and placed it on the cutting board before touching a knife to it. The manner in which he held a peach as he ate it, careful not to bruise its tender flesh.

"You like watching me," he said. "It makes me a little nervous. What are you trying to see?"

Everything, she wanted to say, absolutely fucking everything. After Teddy died, she withdrew inside her house, inside herself. When she re-emerged, she couldn't believe the beauty around her. Family, friends, co-workers, strangers. Sky, trees, lakes. A desire had rooted deep within her to render in paint, pastels, or charcoal the silhouette of a mountain, the shadows on the surface of a creek, a flock of birds arcing up from the grass. She imagined the kind of large swathes of color, the sweep of brushstrokes needed to portray the wide open spaces of the valley below.

Last week Anita watched Perry build a tube for Taggart to run in. She did not like his pet ferret. In fact she was afraid of it. It reminded her of the ferret in *The Big Lebowski*, that dove for The Dude's privates in a bathtub. Taggart's beady eyes made her skin crawl. She had pets as a child, (parakeet, turtle, hamster, spaniel), but she wanted no part of them now.

They required too much care. She wanted to simplify her life, prune it to the things she loved most, things that made her happy: old songs by The Byrds, Cat Stevens, The Animals; long walks in fields near trees and bodies of water.

"Yes, I love watching you measure," she said. "You take your time and you look happy working with your hands. I guess that's why you lay tile for a living."

He stretched his hand out over the valley as if gauging its depth, the stillness of the air, or the vibration level of nearby insects. Her view of the farm below was framed by a semi-circle of wild sumac with ruby-red leaves. Cluster-cones of fleshy fruit reminded her of what she imagined coiled intestines looked like, or exposed chambers of the brain. She moved her gaze beyond the sumac to the rolled bales of hay interspersed throughout the fields.

If Teddy hadn't chosen to work in water rescue, she might have lived on a valley farm like the one below, its white frame two-story with front and back porches shaded by tall, wide trees that looked like sugar maples. Was that a woman sitting in a porch swing? Anita wondered if she'd have been any happier living in the country.

She dragged herself back to the present. To Perry seated beside her. She leaned to press a kiss below his earlobe.

"Did you ever want to live on a farm?" she asked. "It seems like a simpler life."

"Not simpler. Different, harder."

He was often a man of few words, which had taken some getting used to. Teddy had been a talker. A bit of a bullshitter, but in a pleasant, acceptable way.

Perry talked about how much he enjoyed laying tile. Forever fascinated by patterns, and the relation of parts to a whole. As a child, he'd loved math, solving equations, learning formulas, measuring angles, lines, and surfaces.

She asked if he had been afraid of starting his own business at forty-nine. Making decisions was so hard after her husband's death. Anita had never lived alone. She found it both lonely and exhilarating. It took forever to get used to doing whatever the hell she wanted, with no one else to consider.

"I was scared," he admitted. "Everyone said I was nuts, giving up a job with health care coverage, a pension plan, bonuses if you busted your ass."

He swung at a dandelion puffball, releasing its seeds. He related how he broached the subject with his brother Kyle, who'd worked seventeen years for Ohio Tile. He too was ready to start out on his own. At first they barely got enough work to live on. Now, they were able to save a little, not much. "I don't need much to be happy."

Neither did she. At least not financially. Teddy died just short of being vested in his company's pension plan. She'd struggled at first to pay the mortgage of the home they'd built. But once she figured out how to pace her spending to match her income, she decided to sell it and live in a townhouse.

"Don't you worry about retirement?"

"That's what everyone asks." His tone suggested disappointment that she'd joined the ranks of naysayers.

Anita wished she could take back her question.

He ruffled the grass with the palm of his hand. The blades had turned a duller green, edging toward brown. It had been a dry autumn.

"My dad and grandfather tiled until the day they died at seventy-five and eighty. They just worked fewer jobs."

She didn't ask why they wouldn't want to relax, and maybe travel. Slow down and see what they'd missed. The tractor in the field below lumbered with a heavy hum like a bee at the end of its life.

"I have no one to support but myself. No wife, no kids."

No one to take care of you, either, Anita thought. After her husband died she began thinking of her own mortality at the oddest times—doing arm curls at the gym, pruning her bonsai fir, crushing fresh garlic to swirl through hummus.

She was childless also, though she'd had no trouble conceiving. But her three pregnancies ended in miscarriages during the first trimester. They'd made initial inquiries into adoption, but the process seemed too much, emotionally, for Anita to handle at the time. So they settled into their marriage without children. Sometimes she still dreamed of a daughter with Teddy's kind eyes.

Anita had resented when her best friend suggested Teddy had been too protective of her. But had to admit she did not know where the water shutoff valves were located, or how to light the pilot on the furnace, or how to check her oil. Her husband made sure her car's fluids were at the required levels, her tire pressure adequate. She usually ran out of gas twice a year. Teddy always rescued her. He teased her, asking how in the world she managed the thirty employees of the Human Resource Department at Reliance Insurance Company.

"You think you'll ever get married again?" Anita asked.

"No need to."

She turned her head away from Perry, pretending interest in the Holstein cows nibbling in the field to her left. Pouring herself into the plush contrast of black and white. Why did he reply so quickly, so curtly, as if she'd accused him of something shameful? Wasn't it a simple question that merely required a yes or no answer?

She couldn't resist asking, "Not even if you fall helplessly, completely in love?"

"That still doesn't mean I need to get married. I did that once."

Surely he didn't mean you could only do things once in a lifetime? Let it go, she told herself. No need to analyze his every word. Her bad habit of gleaning sinister significance out of things that weren't really that complicated, had worsened after Teddy's death.

"I guess everybody has their own opinions about marriage." Anita spoke slowly, trying not to let any expression jade her words. "Depending on their experience with it." But her voice rose, and the words tumbled beyond her reach. "I had a happy marriage. I'd have no qualms about trying it again."

Perry glanced at her face before saying, "We'll either work together, or we won't. Marriage wouldn't change that."

He never revealed much about his marriage, other than the fact that it lasted less than two years, and involved no children.

Hugging her knees close, she followed the crosshatch line of fencing below. At times it felt as if she'd known him for years. In this moment it became painfully clear how little she knew. They shared so much intimacy in their six months together; yet she feared intruding into areas where she was unclear whether she was welcome or not.

The fields spread out below them, composed of interlocking pieces of a mammoth jigsaw puzzle—varying shades of gold, green, and brown. Every so often, a cluster of trees graced a field, or a lone tree carcass jutted from the ground, bark and branches long gone, struck by lightning, tornado, or old age. She thought about how she'd need to layer an array of gray paints to assemble the weathered barn on the stone foundation, tilting toward the pond.

Anita leaned closer to Perry, ran her thumb and index finger on either side of a crease in his jeans, as if pressing a pleat in place. "Would you mind telling me a little about your marriage?"

"It was a long time ago."

He threw a blade of grass he'd tenderly torn from the ground.

Anita wanted to scream, "How long?" She'd told him everything about her life, held nothing back. Why couldn't he meet her halfway? But she reminded herself that there was no hurry, no need to push so hard. Even though she wanted to celebrate, jump ahead to unbridled bliss. Who knew what might happen to interrupt their happiness?

Her husband had been killed when a boulder from the hillside of an I-275 exit ramp crashed through his windshield. He had been minutes from home, talking to Anita on his Bluetooth. It took her a year before she'd exit on that ramp, travel between the walls which ended twenty years of married life in a few seconds. How many more years would pass before she would not think about that boulder falling?

"She wasn't the woman I should have married." He spoke quietly, as if talking to himself. "I knew it weeks before the wedding, but I didn't have the balls to call it off. All the arrangements were in place. A big ceremony. I didn't have the heart to tell Angie I couldn't go through with it."

He ripped out a handful of grass. "I told myself it was a case of the jitters, perfectly normal, happens to the best of men. But with each day, it became clearer I was making a mistake. A mistake I should in all conscience do something about. But I knew it would break her heart."

His soft-sad voice tore at Anita.

He went on to tell how kind-hearted his fiancé was. She had a good head for business.

She'd started a day-care center and had their whole life mapped out. She wanted two sons and a daughter. They were going to live in an apartment for five years, to save for their dream home.

Layered behind his words was the hum of the tractor. Anita continued to press the fold of his jeans between her thumb and forefinger, from his upper thigh to as close to his knee as she could reach. The heat of his leg soothed her, the way the denim was composed of intricately twined white, black, navy, and blue.

"It's easy to make mistakes when you're young," she said. "Hell, it's easy to make mistakes when you're old." At forty-seven she was just beginning to learn how easy it was to fuck up.

"Maybe you did the honorable thing," she said. "Even though it didn't seem like it at the time. You tried to see it through. Would it have been more honorable to break her heart up front, before you were absolutely sure it wasn't just a case of wedding jitters? What if you called it off and realized later you'd made a terrible mistake?"

He shifted position, so that he leaned away from her slightly. She could no longer play with the fold of his jeans unless she moved closer.

"I don't like talking about the past as much as you do."

Anita felt as if he'd punched her in the gut. She squinted her eyes to concentrate on the pattern of rows the farmer had plowed into the field below. A heavy silence fell. Perry picked up a twisted seedpod and peeled it open. Clear pulp separating the seeds shaped like tiny hearts. She vowed never to bring the subject of marriage up again. Wasn't there some list she could study that revealed taboo subjects never to broach with a new lover? Some text outlining how to navigate a new relationship? She wanted to know him better, but like a person learning to dance, she kept stepping on his toes.

"Lie down," he said. His voice, so intense and serious, scared her. Had he spotted a funnel cloud, a rifle pointed at them?

He spread flat on his back and pointed west of the valley. "Look at that hawk."

Anita wished she'd brought her binoculars. After several minutes of staring at the raptor's graceful sweep—dark against light—the sky and earth inverted. The sky transformed into a huge basin of water. They hung on its underbelly.

"How insignificant do you think we appear to that hawk?" He asked. "And imagine how long this tree's been here. All it's witnessed."

The grass tickled the backs of her legs. Each tree leaf fluttered independently, in its own pattern, together creating a live tapestry.

"There's nothing that makes me happier than looking up into a tree," she said.

"Nothing?" He pinned her to the ground, nuzzling his face into her neck, his tongue flicking the spot that took her breath away.

They'd gone to bed as the full moon rose. Anita couldn't get to sleep. She woke Perry at one-thirty a.m. He grumbled at first, but joined her to slip on hiking boots and thick white full-length terrycloth robes, bare beneath. They'd packed them to use for the outdoor hot tub. With a wide-beam flashlight, they wound their way through the woods, preceded by the fuzzy halo of light. Darkness magnified the whoosh of wind in trees, the snap of twigs underfoot, the rustle of something rooting through underbrush. They walked slowly, savoring every minute. The temperature had fallen through the sixties.

He veered the flashlight to the left, searched the clearing. "Look at your puffballs now."

They had shrunken in on themselves, like something rotting from within.

"The dinosaur eggs are hatching," she insisted.

He rolled his eyes. She couldn't understand why he couldn't play along. Was she asking too much?

The wind kicked up. A crash sounded nearby. Perry swung the flashlight beam into the trees. A stag froze in its tracks, fifteen feet away, headed toward them. Its antlers spanned four feet. She drew in a sharp breath at almost the same time the animal snorted. Goosebumps rose on her arms as he lunged away from them, hooves thudding the ground.

Neither spoke for a minute.

"Sometimes I'm so happy I'm afraid I'll burst," she said.

"The heart is as big as you let it be," Perry said.

He sometimes threw out the most provocative statements. At first she'd felt compelled to answer or challenge them. Lately, she'd learned to let them go, just as they were. Not everything needed a reply.

Listening to the night sounds, they did not speak again until they exited the woods into the open field. The light of the full moon washed over them.

At the lake they sat on a wide flat boulder near shore. She watched weeping willow shadows shimmer on the water's surface. Frog and cricket cries glutted the air. A fish shattered the water's mirror with a plop. Anita closed her eyes and concentrated. She heard the water flow, pictured the outward echo pattern.

Without thinking she whispered, "Teddy used to say no one could look into a lake and not be happy."

Perry did not respond. The silence felt as if it could tear the moon from the sky.

She opened her eyes. Looked across the water to the willow and its wavering shadow.

He placed his hand on hers. "I wonder if you gave yourself enough time to get over Teddy?"

It surprised her that Perry spoke her husband's name. The word sounded dark and sweet on Perry's lips. She wanted to kiss him. Taste her husband's name there.

She turned to Perry, her eyes glassy as the lake. "I waited two years."

"Maybe that wasn't long enough, for you."

He leaned to kiss her forehead. Shivers ran through her. Was he letting her go?

Something pierced the lake's surface. Concentric waves traveled toward her. He nuzzled his chin on her shoulder. Whispered, "Last one to the top of the hill is a rotten egg."

He left her on the boulder, bolted along the lakeshore. The tail of his white robe flailed behind him like a flag of surrender.

She ran after him, screaming his name into the wind loud as she could, entered the open field, headed for the crest of the hill. It felt so good to run. Stretch her legs. Open her lungs and heart. Her throat, larynx, the muscles of her mouth pulsed, bathed in heat. With each breath she sucked in the sweet-sour mash of fresh mown grass.

Ten feet ahead, he unfastened his robe. She opened hers. The cool air lapped her skin. She imagined a long train of white ermine fluttering behind her. Perry slowed. She grabbed the tail of his robe, whipped it off him, and let hers fall away. They ran naked beside each other to the crest of the hill. He lifted her off the ground and brought her down for a kiss, which did not last long. They were out of breath.

Anita twirled around on her toes. Moon shadows of branches on Perry's shoulders looked like tiger stripes. She pictured herself rising, hatching from the earth's axis, her past falling away in loose particles of soil.

Naked

They were going to a nudist camp. Jody held her breath as her boyfriend Monroe drove alongside Spruce Mountain toward a curve where the road disappeared. She knew he was a careful driver. In their two years together he'd handled the backroads of the seven states radiating out from their home state of Kentucky. As he maneuvered around the bend, another panorama spread out before them. The Bluestone River snaked through the valley where small farms nestled between thick forests and an occasional small town. She leaned her head out the window and inhaled the air, trees, and soil.

She followed their progress along the yellow-highlighted line Monroe had charted on the map in her lap. Men and their maps, she smiled to herself. They overflowed the top drawers of his file cabinet. Anytime they stopped at a rest area, he gravitated to their maps. She smoothed her hand over the crisp folds. Roads, towns, rivers, mountains arranged on the grid with its legend illuminated. The West Virginia mountains gave way to hills then flatlands on the way to the ocean. As the miles decreased between them and their destination, The Garden of Eden in Virginia, Jody wondered if her queasy feeling meant anticipation or nervousness. She'd wanted to experience nudism for years, but no one she knew seemed interested. Until she met Monroe.

He wore his hole-in-one cap, inseparable from it since the achievement a month earlier. Jody surprised him by sewing a hole-in-one patch to the hat. She didn't share his love of golf, but listened to his play-by-play, happy for him. Wearing a hat, he looked younger than fifty. His light brown hair had receded until only a few wisps remained on top. He kept the sides and back trimmed short, making it appear thicker.

Monroe asked if she was getting excited. She answered yes, saying she felt a rush like you get when a plane lifts off the ground.

"So, you are nervous," he said.

She replied no, a little too fast. Monroe teased her about looking a little green, saying they could change their minds and go on to Virginia Beach and Jamestown instead. She smiled, slightly irritated at his suggestion that she might want to back out of their plans. Didn't he know by now she couldn't resist a dare? Hadn't she walked several nights with him nude through the cemetery near their house, to get a taste of it? Wearing a wrap around dress with nothing beneath, clothes she could throw on at a moment's notice. She'd practiced in the gym's locker room, amazed at the rigmarole women, teens, and even girls as young as ten performed so no one saw them naked. It was only the youngest children who enjoyed running around the room bare-bottomed. Why were people so afraid of nakedness?

Jody's stomach lurched again, and for a second she wondered what morning sickness felt like, but quickly told herself she was not pregnant. At her annual gynecological visit in the spring, the doctor said her blood work showed her still pre-menopausal. Her periods had remained regular, until now. She smoothed her hand over her abdomen, and asked Monroe if it looked pouchy. He teased, asking if she meant more pouchy than normal. Jody smacked his leg, reminding him she didn't look that bad for forty. She tried not to let her mind wander to anything but the breathtaking view unfolding before them. She recognized white pine, pin oak, and shagbark hickory as the van climbed. Monroe pointed out hemlock, mulberry, balsam fir. He'd inherited the family landscape business. Everywhere they went he taught her how to identify various species. She'd always loved trees, but only knew the easy ones like sycamore, blue spruce, and maple.

Monroe caught her eye and winked. "You're not still worried about being pregnant, are you?"

"No," she lied.

"How late are you?"

"Three weeks."

He asked why she hadn't made a doctor's appointment to find out before they left on vacation.

"Because I'm not pregnant." She hadn't meant her voice to sound so sharp.

Monroe kept his eyes on the road.

I am not going to let this ruin our trip, Jody told herself. She glanced at the van's clock: 11:58. She'd allow herself the two minutes before noon to play out the what-ifs. What if she was pregnant? She couldn't accept abortion or giving a child up for adoption. Monroe might choose to marry her. She loved him, but wasn't sure she wanted to be married. They could continue to live together and raise their child or she could raise the child on her own. Surely she was capable, even if it wasn't her plan. What she never anticipated might present the greatest joy.

Her time was up. As they approached another crest of the mountain road, she pulled the binoculars from the console compartment between them. They topped the mountain and descended. Another valley spread out before them. So many shades of green. She couldn't wait to get in the woods, to ingest their opulence. The Garden of Eden contained a Jacuzzi, a lake, and was within twenty miles of the ocean. Anticipation flushed through her as she imagined herself nude, immersed in water.

Mountains stacked one behind the other on the horizon—purple, blue, and gray—beneath a sky striated by gold veins of sun breaking through. She took a deep breath, let go of all but the countryside. Was there anything as beautiful as wide open land? Monroe caught her gaze and grinned. She raised the binoculars to her eyes to cover pooling tears.

Monroe stood inside the cabin, near its door. "Are you ready?" Jody took a deep breath, and nodded. Naked, they stepped outside. The Blue Ridge Mountain breezes from the west and the Atlantic breezes from the east tickled her skin. Mature shade trees graced the campsites. Monroe pointed out loblolly pines, chestnut oaks, black willows. They passed several campsites where nude adults, teenagers, and children set up tents and pop-up campers, attended grills, and pitched horseshoes. They'd rubbed on sunscreen before leaving the cabin, though from the look of clouds amassing, complements of tropical storm Allison, they wouldn't need it.

She couldn't believe she was finally walking around naked. She thought about the scar from her kidney stone surgery and the abundance of moles distributed over her body. In the small of her back a glazed area remained from the dark, furry mole the dermatologist removed when she was fifteen. She shivered, remembering the mole shaped, sized, and colored like a cockroach. As a young adult, she worried about how much her thighs jiggled when she walked in a bathing suit or shorts. Lord knows what all was jiggling now, she thought.

They headed for the Garden of Eden's office. Monroe stopped alongside a river birch, touching its cinnamon-red peeling bark. A sign "Welcome to the 2001 Eastern Naturist Gathering" hung on the door. A man stood behind the counter, striking keys on a computer. Jody assumed his bottom half was naked as his top, but couldn't verify it unless she leaned and peeked over the counter. He gave them a map of the campground and hiking trails, went over the ground rules, and moved away from the counter to pull their meal tickets from a file cabinet. Yes, he was naked.

She kept her gaze straight ahead, telling herself she would not be embarrassed, trying not to smile. Above his coccyx bone there was an indentation where the skin shone as if a quarter hovered there. She fought the urge to giggle. When he turned back, she saw a long scar down his belly. Gall bladder surgery, she suspected, remembering her mother's similar scar. She moved her eyes level with his, seeing his privates peripherally. Again she struggled not to laugh, thinking how silly sexual organs looked.

Monroe wanted to see if they had any water floats for sale. Jody's nipples hardened when she passed an air-conditioning vent. She resisted covering herself with her arms. A young woman nearby was stocking shelves, her back to Jody. A lizard tattoo decorated one cheek, the other a snake, and a dragon above her tailbone. When she turned to them, Jody tried not to stare. The woman's belly protruded in a mound above her shaved privates. A spider tattoo webbed the top of one breast. Jody envied her radiant, unblemished complexion. Breakouts plagued her teenage and early adult years. No amount of makeup could cover the scars.

She reminded herself that she'd sworn off comparing herself to other women. Part of why she wanted to experience a nudist camp was to let go of any lingering concerns over her body image. Jody couldn't think of a single female friend that could honestly deny they were still cursed with body image issues. How ridiculous, she thought, at her age to be struggling with what she looked like. For once and all, she wanted to be happy in her skin.

"Your first child?" Jody asked the woman, feeling her face redden.

"No, she has an older sister." She extended her hand. "I'm Trillie."

A naked tow-headed toddler came from behind the counter. "This is Morgan."

The child had her mother's silver-blonde hair and light blue eyes. She patted Trillie's belly.

"Do you have any children?" Trillie asked.

"No." And don't want any, Jody thought. She had been pregnant once, in her first year of marriage.

Monroe studied Jody's face, trying to gauge her reaction, she suspected. He told the woman that this was Jody's first time at a nudist camp. Trillie said she remembered her first time, that it was hard not to check out everyone's parts. Don't worry, she said, it's a natural curiosity. People understand. They all had a first time.

As they left the office, Jody remembered the scene she'd walked into a week earlier. Her niece had invited her over to look at baby pictures. When she hadn't answered the bell, Jody tried the door, and walked into the living room. Cara lay on the couch with her infant girl snuggled to her chest, both asleep. Their beauty took Jody's breath away. Tears filled her eyes as she listened to their breathing.

Monroe took her hand as they walked toward the pool. She tried not to wonder what it would be like to have a child. Certainly her life would be totally different. Would she be happier?

The pool area was crowded. At one end a woman soaped herself at an open-air shower. An elderly man had skin so wrinkled it looked as if he wore clothes that had been bunched in a ball for years. Jody noticed a tan middle-aged man stretched out in a lawn chair with a bunched-up beach towel draped over his midsection. Monroe whispered that the man had a hard-on. Said it happened to him the first couple camps he visited. After a while you get used to seeing people naked, he said, and you don't even notice.

"Who you shitting?" Jody teased. "I saw the way you were checking out that blonde in the office. And don't say you were only interested in her tattoos."

Monroe smiled in reply.

Swimming naked felt natural and decadent. Churned-up water tickled between her legs when she lapped the pool. Monroe snuck up from behind and goosed her. She grabbed him underwater. Children, teens, and adults jumped off the springboard—breasts and penises bouncing. One man floated an infant boy on the water's surface. The child kicked his arms and legs. His squeals of delight reminded Jody of the sounds Monroe's grandson Thompson made when he was dragged down in a tickle-fest. The man and child had caught Monroe's eye as well. Did she imagine his jaw tighten? Was he hoping to God she wasn't pregnant?

Jody watched Monroe practice freestyle across the pool's width, struggling to breathe and keep his legs from sinking. They remained muscular from years of martial arts. Almost drowning when young, he carried a phobia of water into his adult life. Six months earlier, he'd completed adult swim lessons at a local high school. He'd made it a priority to see that his grandkids learned to swim at an early age. Jody had learned to swim at the age of five, competing in meets throughout her teen years into her mid-twenties. Until she miscarried.

Before the "Naturist Photography in Nature" workshop began, Jody and Monroe signed release forms, stating they agreed to have their pictures taken and possibly printed in The Naturist Society's monthly publication. The workshop consisted of ten men, Jody and another woman. The leader was a small man, beard tinged with gray. Thick dark hair covered much of his body. He would not meet Jody's eyes, stealing sideway glances at her and the other female. This one's trouble, Jody thought.

The leader said they'd better get to it. Looked like rain. "We'll warm up on the swing set."

Jody watched the other woman, who looked about thirty-five, arrange a towel on a swing before sitting. She pushed off and began pumping her legs. The leader shot pictures of her from various angles. The male participants moved forward, sluggish at first. When the woman smiled and opened her legs a little wider, the men gathered closer, as if drawn by a magnet. She had a Caesarian scar, and large, loose breasts. Throughout the years, Jody wished she had larger breasts, but felt conflicted, as if she were playing into the hands of those who assessed women by the size of their breasts. Silently she'd judged those who resorted to surgical augmentation.

Now for the woods, the leader said. As they walked, Jody pretended not to notice several men getting hard. The leader stopped in front of a large maple. Its trunk divided seven feet from the ground. He asked the younger woman to climb up into the crook. Jody would have told the man to fuck himself. The woman stepped on rungs of wood nailed to the tree trunk, vestiges of a long-gone tree house. Several men steadied her with palms on her rump. She squealed. The leader snapped several photos of her climbing.

"That's cheating," she cooed. "I wasn't ready." She positioned herself in the tree's fork.

The air felt clogged and heavy. No one spoke but the man in charge. "Okay now, strike your pose."

The woman leaned against one branch, her arm around it like the shoulder of a lover, her other arm behind her head. The position resulted in one breast squashed against the tree, the other riding high. Jody stood back a ways, thinking someone should tell the woman she looked deformed. The men circled below, clicking away. Monroe stood back, not too close to the clump of men, but not too far away. Jody's face felt hot, her underarms wet.

They helped the woman down. Jody followed the pack onto the lawn in front of the clubhouse. The leader instructed the woman to get down on all fours and do whatever felt natural. Jody wanted to gag.

The leader lay down on the grass and took side shots of the woman. Her breasts hung like sacks of apples. She arched her back, raising her ass. The other men moved in, jockeying for position. Monroe stood at the back, camera raised to his face. Jody wanted to yank him away.

She left, moving as fast as she could. When she reached the gravel road that wove through the campground, she dug her shoes in. By the time Monroe caught up with her, she'd stomped all the way to the woods at the far end of the campground, working out most of the tightness from her legs and spine. He fell into step with her, not speaking. It had begun drizzling.

"All done with your class?" she asked, as if truly interested.

"Pretty much." He brushed his hand against hers, testing the water. When she didn't pull away, he took her hand. "What did you expect? Did you think we were going to just photograph nature?"

"No. The poster stated clearly it would be naturist photography in natural settings. But it shifted quickly to being sexual and exploitative."

"That woman knew exactly what she was doing," Monroe said, "And exactly what the men were doing. No one took advantage of her. That was the most attention she'll probably get in her lifetime. She ate it up."

"That's beside the point. Those men acted as if they were honing their photographic skills, and all the while they were getting off on it. And you said naturism wasn't about sex or perversion."

"It's not supposed to be," Monroe said. "But people are human."

"And you were in that pack of drooling idiots snapping away."

"Okay, hey, it's a guy thing. If it makes you feel any better, I didn't take any pictures of her. I only pretended to."

"Why?" Jody asked. "Scared to walk away?" She snapped her towel and landed a solid slap to his ass. He rubbed it, pretending it didn't hurt. "What I want to know is why they assumed it had to be women posing for men, and of course they were only interested in the female with the biggest bazooms."

"So you're really mad because they weren't taking pictures of you?"

"No, if that pervert asked me to pose, I'd suggest someone take a shot of me ramming his camera up his ass." Jody couldn't believe the venom in her voice, or the intensity with which she wanted to kick something.

Monroe began to laugh, but turned it into a cough. After walking for a while more, he suggested they not let one jerk spoil their fun. They entered the trailhead of the "Full Moon Trail," joking about the aptness of its name. Monroe picked a blue berry from a red cedar, showing her its waxy covering. He brushed his fingers through the cedar needles, wafting the fragrance under her nose. They enjoyed several slow kisses beneath the canopy of trees.

He pointed to the green fruit of a pawpaw tree, saying raccoons, opossums, and squirrels ate them. Picking up one of its ten-inch oval leaves, he told her he'd read they were the sole food source for caterpillars of zebra swallowtail butterflies. His deep, yet tender voice reminded her of the time he'd shown his grandson how to identify tulip-poplars while on a fall hike at Burlington Bluffs. The four-lobed leaf, he'd explained, looked like a person's body—the two upper lobes the arms, the two lower the legs.

When a downpour started, they hurried for their cabin. The rain beat an entrancing staccato on its tin roof. They wrapped their arms around each other, and rolled back and forth on the bed, laughing. They woke from a post-lovemaking nap, made a picnic on top of the bedspread. Pulling out food from the small refrigerator and their coolers, they fed each other grapes, strawberries, blueberries, almonds, pistachios, and cubes of sharp Cheddar between sips of Chardonnay. The rain continued to ding the roof.

They read for a while in bed—him Bill Bryson's *A Walk in the Woods*, her Barbara Kingsolver's *The Prodigal Summer*. Their bedside window ajar allowed them to hear the crisp sound of raindrops on leaves, bark, and grass. When Monroe hugged her, Jody's breasts felt tender. A wave of heat and nausea spread through her. She couldn't shake the idea that it might be morning sickness.

"What if I'm pregnant?"

He laid his book aside and re-arranged the pillows against the headboard.

"I am not having a child. I'm forty years old." She hugged her knees to her chest. "It's risky to have a child at my age. And what teenager wouldn't be embarrassed by a mother in her fifties?" She struggled to keep her voice calm.

"They might keep you young."

Jody noticed he didn't say a child might keep "them" young. She dug her heels into the bed. "Do you want to become a father again at the age of fifty?"

"Why are you yelling at me?"

"You better not have got me pregnant. I'm not ready for a child."

"This would be a very small world if people waited until they were ready. You'd do fine."

Again, no mention of helping her. Surely, if she was pregnant, he'd accept his part of the responsibility. But what fifty-year-old man wants to begin raising a child?

I need some exercise after all that food," Jody said. "We've been lying around like slugs."

Monroe followed her outside. The soft drizzle tickled her skin. The dregs of dusk gave way to darkness as they walked. Jody's favorite time of day. Sounds magnified and the air felt liquid thick with anticipation. Despite the camp's sand base, water pooled everywhere, ankle-deep in some places. Some of the tent campers, beaten-down looks on their faces, pulled up stakes, packed waterlogged equipment, and headed for home.

The Jacuzzi was deserted. They slipped into its water. The drizzle turned into another downpour, beating the tin roof overhead. Monroe positioned himself so that a water jet hit the small of his back, one of his trouble spots. He asked how Jody was enjoying their naked vacation so far.

"I love it," she replied. "I knew I would. I've been waiting years to do this. I had no idea how many different varieties of breasts there were. And nipples—tiny, large, flat, some like plump raisins. And penises. It's a smorgasbord."

When she'd turned forty, she'd decided to devote the rest of her life to having fun. She'd enjoyed a twenty-year career as a computer technician. Her plan was to coast through the next fifteen years, and retire at fifty-five. She'd probably work part-time at a bookstore, florist shop, or travel agency to augment her pension, so she could travel.

They scooted onto the rim of the Jacuzzi to cool off awhile. Jody tickled her fingertips over the age spots on his palm. He pressed a soft kiss against the inside of her wrist.

Other men filtered in. Brief exchanges ensued, not more than a few sentences—inquiring where they lived, what other nudist camps they'd visited. Four men besides Monroe, their age range from early forties to late fifties. After their second cool down, Jody and Monroe slid back in.

A woman in her early thirties joined them. A small baby slept in a snuggy against her chest. The woman sat on the Jacuzzi step, only her lower torso submerged. Her auburn hair, long and thick, fell in perfect waves onto her shoulders. Jody wondered if she could get away with growing her hair long again. She'd worn it short for the past ten years, even with the bottom of her earlobes. Might be time for a change. Maybe she'd even dye her hair red. She already had natural strawberry-blonde highlights.

Jody wanted to ask about her baby, but didn't want to disturb them. The woman wrapped her arms around the baby and closed her eyes. They seemed sealed in a separate, self-sufficient world like a kangaroo's pouch. She wondered if the woman was a single parent, or the child adopted. Surely she couldn't have given birth a few months ago. Not an ounce of fat remained on her body or a single spider vein on her thighs. Jody had several near each knee. They weren't painful, only unsightly. Several friends underwent a simple procedure where a doctor injected a solution into the veins to collapse them. Eventually they faded from sight. Jody hadn't decided how she felt about all the ways to camouflage a person's age.

She chided herself for comparing herself to the woman, assessing them both against some scale of perfection. When would she and the whole damned world break out of this mold of judging women by their appearance? This nude vacation was supposed to be her last step in letting go of such betrayals.

They'd been in the hot water way too long. Monroe looked red.

"Your face looks like it's going to explode," Jody said. "We better get out. This might be too much for a man your age," she teased, close so only he could hear.

He flipped her off behind his towel, winking.

Passing one of the campsites, they saw a father, under a dining tarp, show his son how to light a kerosene lamp. Jody was reminded of the time she watched Monroe show his granddaughter Kelsey how to plant tomato seedlings. His deep voice softened, intent on describing in simple terms how to make sure the dirt in the pot remained level with the ground soil, how to carefully tamp the soil around the plant's base, and how to water them so that you didn't flood them. He'd let Kelsey try one, guiding her every step of the way. Jody wondered if Monroe had been as patient a father.

They discovered a mud fight in an open field next to the lodge. Kids, teenagers, and adults on their knees in a mid-calf deep lake slung handfuls of mud at others streaking past. They looked like pied horses, mud-splotched head to foot, pinkish skin showing through here and there. Floodlights extended shadows, giving everything a surreal look.

"Want to join them?" Jody asked Monroe, only half kidding.

They removed their soggy sandals and found a spot where the ground felt especially gooshy. Dropping to their knees, side by side, they dug fingers into the field's soft underbelly, packed mud into some semblance of a sphere before flinging it at the nearest target.

A group ran up and down the field, screeching as through a gauntlet, daring anyone to catch them with mud balls. It didn't take long to deplete a spot of pliable mud, forcing them to find another cache. The skin beneath Jody's nails became increasingly tender from gouging holes in the earth. Their bellies hurt from laughing at themselves squatting naked, playing in mud.

"There's your friend," Monroe whispered.

The man who led the photography workshop headed their way.

"Let's see if I can find some hard-packed clay," Jody said. "To knock him upside the head with."

"What, you don't want to go for his balls?" Monroe asked.

A mud ball smacked Jody's cheek, splattering mud into one eye. She hadn't seen it coming. A woman handed her a towel to wipe the mud off her face. Monroe helped her to the outdoor shower, where she rinsed out her eye until the stinging lessened. A cloudburst started, stinging their skin. They ran for the cabin.

"Is it ever going to quit raining?" Jody unfolded a map on top of the bed. "Virginia is a big state. There has to be somewhere we can go where it isn't raining."

Monroe suggested they wait until morning. Usually she liked the sound of rain on a tin roof, but it had turned into an annoying, inescapable din. She tried to dry herself with one of her sweatshirts. Towels in various stages of wetness hung over chair backs, coolers, refrigerator top, empty boxes, and the door handle.

"What's going on?" Monroe asked.

"I don't know," Jody said. "I'm just out of sorts. I can't stand how damp everything feels. There's nothing left to dry off with." She hated how petty her voice sounded.

He took her hand. "Let's get some sleep before we decide anything."

She curled up on her side against Monroe. Despite his warmth, she couldn't relax enough to fall asleep. After fifteen minutes, she released an exaggerated sigh. Monroe sat up in bed and switched on a light. "Something besides the rain's bothering you."

"I'm not having a child. I'd be a terrible mother. I've already proven that."

"What are you talking about?"

Jody explained how she'd qualified in breaststroke at a nationwide Marlin's swim meet twenty years ago. She was pregnant, eight weeks along, not showing yet. She'd wanted to swim in one last competition, sure nothing would happen to the baby. Her chances to win the gold medal were the best ever. She'd been swimming all her life.

Her voice broke when she told Monroe that her baby miscarried the next morning.

Monroe smoothed his palm down her back as if brushing away the memory. "It might not have had anything to do with you losing the baby."

"But I was so damn selfish to take the risk."

"Maybe you did act irresponsibly; but my God, you were young. You still don't know for sure you're to blame." He soothed his palm over her shoulders.

"That isn't the end of it." She admitted never telling her husband she was pregnant, so she never told him she lost the baby either.

Monroe said nothing. Silence hung heavy as mildew.

She'd realized her husband had a right to know, but told herself that what he didn't know wouldn't hurt him. Afraid and ashamed, she'd started taking birth control pills. One secret led to another. Her shame escalated. Her husband assumed they were working on starting a family.

Monroe's hand pressed against her shoulder blade. Or was he pushing her away? After a while, he whispered, "Don't you think it's time you let that go?"

"I thought I had, until my period was late."

"Maybe this is your second chance."

"I don't want one."

The memory returned of the infant curled in sleep on her niece's chest. Again she wondered what it would feel like to be a mother. She believed she'd resolved the issue years ago. A therapist told her she needed to grieve for her lost child and for not fulfilling her body's imperative to conceive. She'd wanted to scream, "Shouldn't that be a choice?"

Jody had finally told her husband she didn't want children, but by that time the marriage was in jeopardy for other reasons. Would children have grounded them, made them try harder to save their marriage? Kendal was a good man. Would have made a good father. And Monroe?

As she cried, Monroe fit his body against hers, enfolded her like a cocoon. "Jody, I'll help you if you're pregnant. Surely you know that." He kissed the crown of her head, nuzzled the nape of her neck.

She tasted the salt of her tears. After a time, she became aware their breaths had synchronized. She said, "Let's get out of here. I want to see the ocean."

They packed, putting everything wet in garbage bags. For the first time in days, they put on clothes. Jody noticed how comforting they felt, dry and soft.

Monroe tickled his fingers through the hair along her neckline. "I'll back the van closer, and open the back doors, so you won't get as wet."

As Jody heaved the strap of her duffel bag over her shoulder, she felt the sudden surge she'd hoped for—the unmistakable rush of blood. Worry drained from her, but in its place an ache of loss blossomed.

What She Fractured

It began with a plastic-framed handheld mirror, minutes after Skye returned home from her husband's funeral. At fifty-five, Evan had not survived a heart attack. *Myocardial infarction, coronary thrombosis*—words the emergency room doctor gave her.

His coworker, Colin, wouldn't stop telling her the details at the funeral home layout. *Layout*—a horrible term. Everything and everyone on display—*laid out*. Colin went on and on about how, in their company cafeteria, talking, laughing about Trump's latest debacle, Evan had measured off a spoonful of key lime pie, and raised it to his mouth. How his arm fell to the table, the spoon clanged and spun. How he slumped sideways in his chair, and slid to the floor. A woman screamed. Colin tried to straighten him out, listen for a heartbeat. "But he was gone."

Colin had already told her these details of Evan's last few moments alive, when he met her at the hospital. Now, at the funeral home, he zeroed in on the key lime pie, and how much her husband loved key lime pie, as if she didn't know Evan's preferences. She supposed Colin was as nervous as she was, talking to fill the space.

The intense scent of roses and lilies overwhelmed the room. Her arm, her hand tingled. She might slap Colin, if he mentioned key lime pie one more time. Her mouth assumed the bittersweet, sour taste of that damned pie, which she hated and her husband loved. Skye needed silence, she kept thinking, space to breathe, to listen, to wait for what came next, and to see if time enfolded her.

She stood beside the open casket, accepted hugs from people as they streamed past for the viewing. Another barbaric practice, in her opinion. She tried not to look at Evan. Peripherally she glimpsed his pale gray shirt, and his tie striped lavender, mulberry and silver. If only he'd open his lids once more, so she could memorize his eyes—dusky umber.

"Yes, he was sure enjoying that key lime pie," she heard Colin say, a few feet away. "He closed his eyes, as if to taste it better."

She focused on breathing to stop the shivers in her belly. Yes, Evan had a habit of savoring things with his eyes closed, especially when he sipped a good, dry wine, as they had the night before he died. Four days ago.

They'd turned off MSNBC on the TV, nauseated by replays of Trump bragging, and repeating *no collusion* three times, like some goddamned charm, in a rant that neither made sense nor resembled a sentence.

"Alexa," Evan had instructed the voice assistant device, "please play Norah Jones' *Come Away with Me* album on low volume."

Pillows behind their backs at either ends of the couch, ankles touching, they held glasses of Malbec. Opening chords of "Don't Know Why" sounded, followed by the singer's breathy voice. A platter of spreadable gorgonzola and one-inch squares of extra-sharp cheddar lay on the cocktail table within reach. Evan pushed his soles against hers, trying to instigate a foot wrestle.

"Don't make me spill any of this." She luxuriated in the wine's smoky flavor and aroma that suggested dark fruits.

Evan popped a cheddar square into his mouth, and sipped some wine. He closed his eyes, hummed the song's refrain. After a few minutes of silence, he inhaled deeply, and opened his warm brown eyes. "What if we quit our jobs, sold everything, and moved to Europe?"

She shouldn't have been surprised. He watched every episode of HGTV's *House Hunter International*, taking notes and updating a spreadsheet on the most reasonable places to live abroad.

"I've narrowed it down to Prague; Budapest; Oporto, Portugal; Riga,

Latvia; Rijeka, Croatia."

A pain, like panic, like exhilaration, surged in her as her husband slowly enunciated the litany of names, as if each held a particular flavor.

"Ljubljana, Slovenia; Tallinn, Estonia; Saint-Chinian, France; Abruzzi, Italy."

Skye gave no reply. Slid her lids closed. Wandered villages alongside vineyards, the mountains, the sea. *Maybe.*

Skye had raced home from Evan's funeral, everything she'd repressed gagging her. Well-meaning friends and family had whispered she had to *get a hold of herself* when she'd begun full-body weeping and shaking. They feared she wouldn't be able to get through the day. It took her breath away—others telling her how to behave at her husband's funeral. But fury had allowed her to cork the grief for the moment, prevent the consummate weight of her loss to smother her.

As she drove home at dangerous speeds, she disgorged scream after scream, mouth stretched wide open as if to empty herself. She turned onto her street lined with goddamned gorgeous pears, cherries, and magnolias flowering. Their beauty stabbed her.

She retched when she reached their primary bathroom. The sour-sweet stench choked her, buckled her legs. She leaned on the vanity counter, opened the drawer that held fresh washcloths, wanting something cold on her face. A folded square of paper lay atop the sea-green cotton. A chill prickled her arms.

Let's do it! A squiggly "E," Evan's signature. One of his endearing habits, leaving her notes tucked here and there.

Skye grabbed the puke-pink handle of a mirror, lifted it from the counter. She wanted to smash it into the wall mirror before her, entrapping all of her but her legs. Her dark purple dress suggested something raw and slithery broken loose. Her fist tightened around the handle. A salty, metallic taste bloomed on her tongue.

Raising her arm high, she slammed the handheld mirror into the sink. Shards skittered everywhere. Slivers hit her face—one below an eye, one on her cheek near her ear.

"My god, I could have put out an eye."

Her instinct was to grab the mirror to check close-up for a piece embedded in her face. She flung the mirror's empty frame into the garbage can, stared at the array of what looked like stars against the pearl-gray bowl of the sink. Relief washed through her, strong as a sexual release.

"Look at the fucking mess you made."

Skye leaned toward the wall mirror, knocking fragments off the vanity top. Remembering a mirror in her purse, she moved toward the living room. Her heels crunched bits against the tile floor, dragged sharp particles onto the carpet. It took an hour to clean up the debris, a slow and methodical process. A calmness, a euphoria settled around her like a tub of hot bathwater.

All night she dreamt of that mirror, crashing it again and again into the milky gray bowl of the sink that morphed into the plush black urn of night sky. Star specks flashed a message she struggled to decode. She lowered a large chunk of glass to her wrist, poised to tear herself open. Woke with a giddy panic swirling inside her, itching to throw something, to watch it shatter.

In the dining room her eyes fell on the hutch, plates tilted for optimal viewing. Goosebumps rose on her arms. She removed a plate from its niche. She barely remembered the person she had been thirty years ago when they chose the Vintage Tuscan England bone china collection for their wedding registry. As if all her later selves overlaid her young self, a kind of firing process similar to the glaze firing used in the making of bone china.

They rarely used it anymore. She stared at the pattern she had once loved. On a luminous white background, a black vine with lacy leaves cascaded along the rim. Poppies of bright aqua, rose-pink, and yellow with chartreuse tiny leaves. *Bone china*, stamped on the back. So beautiful and volatile her wrists ached, making her think of broken bones. The skeletal system—too many crackable parts.

Bone china, clay mixed with bone ash—crushed cattle bones, milled into fine particles. It sickened her when she read about the ash of cow bones contained in her china. She thought *bone* referred to its white color.

In the kitchen, she balanced the plate in the palm of her hand. So light, so fragile. How upset she was when she broke one of the saucers a few years into their marriage. She'd planned to see if a replacement could be ordered, but never did.

Unease paired with buoyancy in her midriff. When she pulled open the basement door a cool breeze almost made her drop the plate. She stepped down onto the landing, clutched the railing with one hand.

She flung the plate down the stairs. It splintered with a burst eerie as a high-pitched screech—a vibration in her throat. A thin dust rose. Or did she imagine it? She thought again of those cows and the ash of their bones. Her arm and shoulder radiated warmth. It didn't make sense, she knew, pulverizing objects she once cherished. Keepsakes.

She wandered room to room, sweating, weeping, desperate to slam one of the delicate teacups. A pile of empty boxes her sister Myra had dropped off lay by the front door. The dining room table held sympathy cards; a book listing names of all who attended the funeral service; planters and vases of flowers sent by co-workers, neighbors, family and friends.

From a small box, Skye picked up a leftover holy card. The Blessed Virgin Mary silhouetted from the waist up, in a sea of incandescent white lilies. She cradled the baby Jesus. Behind them, a dark sky of splintery stars. On the back, the *Memorare* prayer. Skye recalled her mother reciting those words twice daily for a month—a novena for special intentions, such as when her aunt was diagnosed with breast cancer, or Skye's father with throat cancer. How desperately her mother prayed, believing with all her heart that Mary would intercede to save them.

Skye consumed much of the next two weeks with shattering and sweeping up the remains. She broke the vases and ceramic pots people sent to express their sympathy, and stuffed the plants and flowers into the garbage can. Then she returned to her fine bone china, only allowing herself to break one piece a day. With each plate, saucer, bowl or cup, she shunned lumps of herself.

Sometimes she cried while she cleared away the breakage. But she could not deny how much calmer she felt afterwards, how gratifying she found smashing anything too painful to see. Her wreckage remained a secret. On the basement stair landing she kept heavy leather boots. On a hook, safety goggles. Overkill, because she threw from near the top of the stairs. If she ventured down a few steps, she gripped the railing with one hand while she hurled with the other.

She thought of her demolition as blood-letting, *phlebotomy*, the medieval practice of draining blood to cure illnesses. She didn't want to hurt herself, or she might have turned to *cutting*. She'd been tempted that first time, staring at the sharp dregs of the mirror she'd broken after the funeral. It would have been so easy to choose a larger chunk, to slit her wrist a little.

It scared her how addictive breaking became, but she was careful. When she returned to work, she limited herself to just one binge a day, then one a week at the year anniversary of Evan's death. She settled into her new life as a single woman, met friends for dinner, a movie, play, or concert. She never invited anyone to her house. No one questioned why.

On the second anniversary of Evan's death, Skye decided on saving money to fulfill her husband's proposal of moving to Europe. Sure, it hadn't been her dream, but she accepted it as something she wanted to try for herself—a different kind of breaking. She needed to select a destination. What about Asia or South America? She started watching *House Hunters International*, and updating Evan's spreadsheet.

Her father had worked for a national law firm that required the family to move every few years, so Skye and Myra grew accustomed to leaving friends and making new ones. Upheaval felt normal. Skye had no children. Her only sibling, Myra, had raised her son Orin alone, would never reveal who his father was, at least not to Skye. A year ago, Orin died in a Tennessee wildfire, on vacation with his fiancé. They attempted to outrun the flames. Their truck hurtled over an embankment, their bodies found a hundred feet away. Six months later, Myra married a rich man ten years younger than her. He spoiled her any way she'd let him.

Skye kept two plates of her china intact. The rest she broke, feeling lighter, stronger with each item flung. Her sense of wellbeing and control increased with each release executed. She grew enchanted, obsessed with the sound of delicate china striking the basement floor—intricate as tiny bells or wind chimes, the way it echoed off the cement floor and walls. Every object had its own notes disintegrating—a saucer different than a dinner plate or teacup. She supposed it had to do with weight.

She didn't always clean the broken slivers up right away. She'd waited a month or two before donning thick leather work gloves and boots to sweep the residue into a dustpan, dump it into black heavy-duty, tripled garbage bags, roll the can to the curb. She didn't want anyone to get cut.

Once she'd shattered all their fine bone china except for two plates, she switched to their crystal stemware. Before dropping each piece, she turned them to refract light off their diamond-cut pattern, and extended her arm as if offering Chardonnay to a guest. She set aside two wine glasses, the ones she and Evan had used the night before he died. They'd joked that wine tasted better out of shimmery, expensive crystal. Neither of them knew, or cared about the difference between wine goblets; sherry, margarita, or martini glasses; and champagne flutes.

How little all that mattered. Yes, how fun, to choose and register for all the beautiful fine china and crystal stemware. She'd felt luxurious and sophisticated. But the fun they enjoyed together, their adventures as Evan called them, remained the real keepsakes: climbing Machu Picchu, hiking in the Grand Canyon, (they had the knees to prove it), parasailing in Key West, and white water rafting in a glacial river in Iceland. Evan had even convinced her to zip line in Jaguar Cove, Belize and Costa Rica's Monteverde Cloud Forest Reserve.

When no crystal stemware remained, except for two wine glasses, Skye visited thrift stores, flea markets, and antique malls, looking for chipped china that cost next to nothing. She'd get panicked if she didn't have a surplus of items ready to ruin.

The sound of severing became a kind of music. The finest porcelain clinked, reminiscent of the piercing ring at the far right end of a piano keyboard. If no fine china was available, she hurled heavy stoneware that cracked apart in bigger chunks—a jarring clatter that resembled the abysmal piano keys on the far left. Instead of slamming an object at the floor, sometimes she arced one for the closest basement wall, like a Frisbee. That tone varied slightly from that of concussing the floor. Other times she let a piece slip softly from her hand. But she could not bear to miss its descent, its moment of impact. This notion of anticipating, and participating as witness to the fall, got her musing about the dynamics of falling, and what it felt like to plummet.

One day in her third year of ruin, she bought a Homer Laughlin bluebird plate so exquisite she yearned to keep it for herself—beauty to contemplate when she didn't want to go to work, or when an anniversary caught her off-guard. Three bluebirds viewed from above, wings extended, with the edges of soft pink underbellies visible, matching pink flowers attached to a viney stem linking the three together.

Painted mid-flight, the birds reminded her of the out-of-control tingle of zip lining high above ground, knowing she'd fracture so many bones if she fell. An ache seethed in her, so strong, she feared she might be having a heart attack. She forced herself to send the plate flying, imagined the birds finally set free to ascend into blue, blue sky.

She hadn't purged the remains in a while. Quite a pile had accumulated. She enjoyed stepping on the pieces as she swept. Cracking the already broken created its own unique jangle. Her sweeping raised a powdery film, released a scent redolent of chalk. She wondered if dust contained in particles of cement jarred loose when struck.

As she gathered chips in a dustpan, she remembered the NPR interview about people jumping off the Golden Gate Bridge. They'd talked to an actual survivor. Skye had pulled off the highway, overcome with relief that she never decided to jump off anything. The thought of her bones cracking terrified her. Still, she speculated about leaping—the interval before rupture. What if she'd stepped off a tall building? A bridge, or canyon? What sound would her body make breaking?

Skye rolled the carry-on suitcase to her front door. It held the only things she owned now. Her steps echoed, the house emptied of furniture and carpets. When she completed one last task, she'd call a cab to take her to the airport.

She'd sold her house, car, and wall art. The rest she'd donated to Habitat for Humanity and veterans organizations. She'd quit her job, transferred money abroad. Said goodbye to friends, her sister and brother-in-law. A few promised to visit. Skye refused several offers to accompany her to search for an apartment to rent. She assured them the realtor she'd contacted could handle it.

She'd decided on Prague. To stay a year or two, then maybe move to Budapest or Reykjavik, Iceland.

Skye lifted two plates and two wine glasses from the floor—the remaining physical symbols of her marriage—and headed for the basement. When she opened the door, a sweet powdery aroma met her, especially strong from her intensive sweeping a few hours ago. Now, to compose one last mess.

She set the plates and glasses on the landing. What happiness all those years ago when she and Evan picked out wedding registry items at McAlpin's Department Store—the moment of bliss when her eyes found the intricate pattern she chose to begin their life together.

In each palm she balanced a twin plate. Her gaze followed its lime green leaves, the poppies lemon yellow, magenta, and robin's egg blue. Hugging the curve of the plate's rim, an arched branch reached inky black into bone-white sky. She pressed her lips against its tiny eye-shaped leaves.

She clanged both plates together like cymbals before dropping them. Her fingers vibrated. One plate landed a second before the other in an exquisite burst that echoed through the empty chamber. A gauzy haze rose—a reversal, she mused—a release back to their bone ash.

She cradled the crystal bowl of each wine goblet. The diamond-etched pattern tickled her skin. She closed her eyes, slipped back to the last night of her husband's life, when they held these glasses filled with Malbec. How Evan opened his eyes, pecan brown. Posed the idea of moving to Europe. An odd mix of alarm and arousal flooded her.

She breathed deeply. The musty smell of the basement reminded her of the pungent cheese they'd nibbled—gorgonzola, extra sharp cheddar.

She'd been asleep when he left for work the following morning. When she'd entered the kitchen, the crystal wine glasses lay upside down in the sink. She'd washed them, the fragrance of dish soap fusing with the wine's tang.

Her eyes opened, and she clinked the goblets together, raised them as in a toast. Their shape suggested Catholic chalices believed to hold the symbolic body and blood of Christ.

"Evan," she whispered, before hurling the vessel at the basement wall. The crash sent shivers up her arms. Shards skittered against the floor like the tinkle of a charm bracelet. She imagined Evan preceding her to Prague. She flung the last glass. Breaking herself open one last time.

The Dance

Dewey's fist slams something. In the next room, I feel the force in the soles of my feet. Has my husband finally lost control? His temper's worsened since the death of our son, Neville, five years ago. Our lives should have calmed by now, but Dewey's more tense than ever. Surrounded by strings of outdoor Christmas lights arranged in a rectangle, he is trying to figure out why three-fourths of them don't work. He loaded the light strings onto the porch posts without testing them. Doesn't think before he acts. I pointed this out to him. He said he doesn't have to—he's a man.

One thing I can tell you about my husband is that he loves and hates mechanical things. They bring out the best and worst in him.

Writing Christmas cards at the dining room table, I lean to see him seated on the living room floor. Pisses me off that his hair remains as thick and red as the day I met him, while mine grays and thins. He's also kept his shape: broad shoulders (not stooped) and trim, tight waist. Claims it's because of the heavy equipment he operates. Says I worry too much about what he calls my body "filling out," when it just means I'm softer to touch.

Dewey glances up to Neville's train on the mantel. His posture softens as if he's floating on his back in a lake, cradled by water. I turn away, holding onto this image of him.

An hour ago, before he even pulled the lights out of the box, I said it might be time to buy a few new sets rather than fuck with the old ones. He gave me one of his slant-eyed glances, and said, "Lacey, you know I don't like it when you curse." Mind you, he curses all he likes, but I'm supposed to use words such as "oh shoot," or "fudge." But he hasn't succeeded in cleaning up my mouth in almost three decades. Oh sure, he remains ever hopeful, but by now you'd think he'd know I might be named Lacey, but I'm neither soft nor frilly.

"Well, you cocksuckers." He punches something, maybe the leather couch cushion. It sounds like a blow to someone's muscled midsection.

As I concentrate on addressing an envelope with controlled loops, I try not to think about Dewey spiraling away from me, deeper into the pit of anger. It's no use. I sink into the memory of his violent rage the night Neville was hit. A drunk S.O.B. driving a pickup way too fast, lost control, and barreled onto our sidewalk. Neville had been at a basketball game, and a pizza joint afterward. Struck on his way to the porch. Twenty feet from our front door. Last month the scum that killed our son was released on parole.

I feel another pounding vibration in my gut. Dewey is a simple man, I tell myself. Simple things are important to him. Decorating a tree and stringing outside lights are traditions to him, rituals that keep him anchored. Or maybe he does them to pass the time, or to feel normal. But if you ask me, we ought to string something unusual across the porch— bones, beetles, teeth. Over the years I wore him down with my suggestions to pare down to a smaller Christmas tree. This year he agreed to sit a three-foot silver-blue shimmer tree on the end table. I got tired of the real trees, even the fake real ones. We've advanced to just fake. Why do we even need a tree? Our grown sons rarely come home for the holidays. Company seldom visits. No one sees the tree but us and Santa Claus. Wouldn't it be nice to still believe?

Dewey wants the Christmas cards sent. When I attempt to convince him to let go of the tradition, he always responds "Maybe next year." The address list dwindles each Christmas. I try not to think about the relatives and friends, some our age and younger, who died this year. Dewey lost his friend Bonesy. Feels so sad addressing the envelope to his wife only. My Aunt Virgie died, the last one of that generation, leaving me the oldest Akers. As I age, it gets harder to deal with the death of patients I tend at the nursing home. They have so little left at the end. One woman told me she'd outlived two husbands, her daughter and son, all her friends. Every night she prays for the sweet release that will allow her to join her loved ones.

"You dirty little bastard." Another bash.

Nothing brings out Dewey's temper like something he can't fix. I steer clear of him when he's riled up by something mechanical or electrical. I'm used to people with bad tempers. I had one as a child. My dad tried to beat it out of me. I bashed in many a plywood door with my running shoes. Why waste all that cushion and shock absorption on running? I had nowhere to go. There's nothing like the satisfaction of feeling the crunch of wood giving way. It was worth the beating I got. He couldn't hurt me. I went right out of my body and watched that old man sweating and breathing hard, swinging that belt as if it was going to change anything. Eventually I outgrew my temper tantrums, after I began to see how silly and sad Dad looked during his rages.

Dewey hammers his fist on the floor, rattling the glass in the window behind me. You might find it hard to believe, but my husband is a spiritual man. He believes things eventually work out; things right themselves. If you're patient, life comes back around, like the boomerangs he bought our sons. He told them boomerangs were invented in the Stone Age, and exactly how they work is still a mystery. Dewey believes in the power of things repeated. He's like one of those fine-oiled machines he maneuvers for a living—the wrecking ball that arcs back and forth again and again, leveling the old, making way for the new.

Years ago I nicknamed him Boomer. He thinks it's after Boomer Esiason, a former Cincinnati Bengal player, but it's short for Boomerang. Dewey shoots way out on a tangent, but he always curves back home. I don't want to think about the time he almost didn't. Two years after Neville's death, Dewey told me something had to change. My drinking had to stop, or he was leaving. He said he'd never been unfaithful, but lately he'd wanted to. Didn't know how much longer he could wait for me to come back to life. Scared the crap out of me that night. I couldn't imagine life without him. He wanted his wife back, he said, the Lacey he married. At that time,

I no longer remembered her.

One thing I can tell you about my husband is that he throws his soul into whatever he's working on at the moment. Like puzzles. He loves to build jigsaw puzzles. A bundle of nervous energy, he works them standing up, dancing around the table when we near the end. We spread the pieces out on the dining room table, its only use in years. The puzzle we're working on now is an aerial view of a tango festival in Argentina. I scooted it carefully down the other end of the table from where I spread the Christmas cards. Every so often I glance at the jewel-toned costumes—all that controlled motion. The cardboard smells dry and dusty, erotic. The sound puzzle pieces make when you sift through them soothes me.

I love watching Dewey study the edges of puzzle pieces, memorizing the necessary shape of a desired piece as he shuffles through the pile, searching for a match. He likes panoramic landscape puzzles—foreign places we fantasize visiting before we die: The Cliffs of Dover, the giant stone monoliths on Easter Island, Chateau de Versailles. I prefer canines playing poker, a maze of famous eyes, or skeletons at a tea party. We have one rule: You can't put an inner piece in place until you complete the border. We divide the pieces into the top and bottom of the puzzle box. Each of us shuffles through our box of approximately equal pieces, ferreting out the border. Once we complete the frame, we race to see who gets to the middle first. Suspense rises as we work towards each other, Dewey in the clouds, me in the fields.

The living room turns way too quiet. I lean in my chair to see. The lights remain stretched around the room, but Dewey's missing. He must have gone into the bedroom. But why didn't he say something?

Oh, but I can handle this. I'm used to tiptoeing around people, knowing when to get out of their hair, when the air in a room sours, and when I better do something quick. Entering the living room, I turn on the stereo, find a channel with instrumental Christmas songs. Standing by the hallway leading back to the bedrooms, I sing as loud as I can the first lines of my own versions: "All I Want for Christmas is a Good Hard Man," "I'm Dreaming of a Ride for Christmas," and "Deck the Halls with Tubes of Joy Gel." Maybe my humor will catch him off guard, relax him. Or give me a slight edge, maybe just a few seconds, to figure a way to get him free of his anger. But sometimes humor backfires.

Dewey loves one thing as much as I do—silk. So I shouldn't be surprised when he enters the hallway wearing only his dark-plum silk robe. There's nothing like a man swaddled in dark silk. He asks me to dance. Wraps his arms around me, and off we sail, marking off the borders of the dining room, the living room.

Relax, I tell myself, slide into the sound of violin, cello, bass. The vibrations build upon each other. Time and space flatten. Nothing matters when I dance with Dewey. I was a terrible dancer when we met. Wound tight as a drum, it took years to relax enough to let the music and Dewey lead me. He loops me along with him, and we leave all life's idiocies behind. Some couples make up after a fight by making love. We dance our way back into each other's graces.

At eighteen he had a chance to go to California with his uncle to start a dance studio. His uncle died a millionaire from stringing along old maids, lonely widows, and geeks—making them believe if they only knew how to dance, their luck in love would change. He asked Dewey to go with him. But our relationship was getting serious, and he'd just started training to be a crane operator, which really intrigued him. So he passed. Dewey never expressed any regrets, but I wonder. If he could go back and make the decision over, would he choose the same?

He feels stiff tonight. Probably from being on the floor so long, messing with those lights. His tension travels, lodges in the small of my back. When he laces his fingers through mine, the pads of our palms meet. Though his calluses nudge me like knots, our extended hands serve as a rudder. We certainly need guidance. I'm bone-tired of living blind. Feeling my way back to where we dovetailed.

Dewey checks how close we come to the rectangle of Christmas lights on the floor. With his foot, he scoots them out of the way, not missing a step. He observes things closely, from the tiniest operations of an ant carrying crumbs or a worm tunneling through soil, to things like a snake shedding its skin or our cat Lucille licking herself clean, to waterfalls, ocean waves, and implosions. We found a rolling ball sculpture in Forest Fair Mall, a thirty by fifteen-foot perpetual motion machine. Dewey designed plans to build his own. Wanted to remove a wall to open up an area large enough to contain it. Starting into things exhilarates him. My dear Boomer scurries around like one of those balls in the perpetual motion machine. He sees gravity as the epitome of grace—precise, simple, and so inevitable, so reliable. If only life were that way.

With the slightest pressure between my shoulder blades, Dewey guides me. The strain in his arms resembles a rubber band about to snap. I breathe in the elemental scent of him. When we first met, he'd tried to cover up the smell of his job's machinery. Until I admitted to liking the way his work settled on his skin—ore and oil from deep in the earth.

There's something especially tender about Dewey's hold on me tonight. The thought no sooner formed, I realize the room's air has soured. As we orbit the living room, the certainty that he is keeping something from me reverberates from the tips of my toes to the top of my scalp. Something is not right, and he's afraid to tell me.

I turn my thoughts to the way we used to spend evenings. How we snuffed every light, laid on our backs in bed, and watched tiny pinpoints of red, blue, green, purple, and gold of a motion light swirl the ceiling. Sometimes he played a CD of piano pieces by Nancy Rumbel or Liz Story, following along with his fingers on an imaginary keyboard. He could have been one hell of a musician. I remember the way he loved to talk about the progressions of notes—the way they mingle and repeat and come full circle. He sang in a voice that always surprised me—deep yet light, simple but rich like the tunes he chose: "Tupelo Honey," "Water Boy," "Blueberry Hill."

As we whirl around the room's edges, desire sparks and radiates. But twined with it is the weight of his strain, his effort to conceal and control. I move my mind to the way our bodies align. We're mirror images. Thin, fine hair covers his chest, arms, and legs, but the hair on his head is thick and full. My arms and legs host the hair of a man, but the strands on my head hang fine and thin. Our bare feet make sounds against the cool, hardwood floors—one of the projects Dewey actually finished after years of nagging. Wide oak planks with a hint of amber.

He enjoys working with tools. When he picks one up, he tells me its name, turns it as he describes its purpose, and places it in my hand, smiling, as if there's nothing finer than seeing his wife hold a prick punch, needle-nose pliers, or ratchet screwdriver. Of course men named tools— spreader, driver, nailer, grinder, drill, shank, nuts, nibbler, stud sensors, biscuit jointers.

The pain in the crook of my back has spread to my hips. We've been dancing for fifteen minutes. I want to get off my feet, but I don't dare abandon Dewey. He's mulling something over, like the motion of water over stone.

Gliding together, his hand slides to the top of my rump. Except for the calluses, his hands are soft. They used to crack and bleed in the winter, until I began massaging them nightly with almond oil. Which usually turns into foreplay. To me, hands are the most sexual part of a man. And I swear the fragrance of almond is an aphrodisiac.

Dewey dips me toward the fire until my scalp prickles. When we sweep past the front door, goosebumps rise on my arms. A harp version of "Greensleeves" begins, and we hum in unison. The vibrations tickle my throat and the drum of my ear pressed against his chest. Maybe the coming year will settle us back into the happiness we once enjoyed. Time we finally put our son's death behind us. We're never going to get better if we continue to drag him along. Maybe we'll travel more to visit our other sons and grandkids. Michigan, Virginia, and Georgia aren't at opposite ends of the earth from Kentucky. We used to have the best conversations on long country drives. Dewey enjoys driving. A car, after all, is a machine he can analyze. I run my fingers through his hair, wondering if we have the energy to start over. Releasing a deep sigh, I acknowledge to myself the truth that we haven't really been living since Neville died. Just going through the motions like the gravity machines that fascinate Dewey.

The stress in his arms spikes. He clamps me in one of his vises, desperate to keep us together, anchored. I try not to imagine what he doesn't want to tell me. He's not someone who keeps secrets. Unless. I miss a step, but Dewey compensates, and catches us back in sync. No, we've had enough heartbreak. Let the wrecking ball fall on some other poor sucker. For now, I pretend not to know anything has changed. Force myself to act as if everything will be okay, as I've done countless times. My hand rests against his carotid artery. Such a strong pulse. A wave of gratitude sweeps through me for all the times Dewey supported me. When he proposed, he said he would love me until I could love myself.

In the midst of Christmas tunes, the radio station throws in a spiritual. "Amazing Lace," He sings near my ear. "How sweet the sound."

His voice curls my toes. The sound echoes through him into me.

"I once was lost, but now am found." His fingers thrum against the blades of my shoulders, as if to activate wings. "Was blind, but now I see."

Eyes closed, I follow Dewey's lead, hoping if we whirl and spin we'll somehow circumvent whatever happened, whatever will happen, whatever he's afraid to reveal. How much longer can we dance?

Our motion past the fireplace stokes the sweet smoke scent. We spiral through the rooms of the home we've shared for so long. I barely hear. My world collapses to only our synchronized motion. Thump of his blood against my fingertips. Heat of his skin through the sea of silk.

His voice wavers, as if he might break into tears, but it deepens into the finale. "When we've been there ten thousand years, bright shining as the sun, we've no less days to sing God's Lace, than when we first begun." Again he leans me toward the fireplace. The crackling's so close, for one crazy second I think he wants to catch me on fire. But he sweeps me back up, an unforgettable sensation of surging through layers of time and place. Everything but the pleasure of the dance falls away from me, and I emerge newly-formed as from a cocoon.

He carries me to the couch, pulls me into his lap, my back against his chest, so we can't see each other's face. Here it comes, I warn myself. I delay by asking him to tell me a story.

He rests his chin on top of my head, his arms encasing the length of me.

"Lacey."

His deep, sweet voice wraps around my name like a special gift that only I can open, at only this moment.

"I have cancer. There are tumors on my spine, my ribs, in my lungs and liver."

The wrecking ball blindsides me, dead in my center, deep into my kidneys. All this time I thought it was Neville, or the Christmas lights. Please God, let it be the lights.

I buck and curse but he holds me until I go limp. He pulls the afghan off the back of the couch, smoothes it around me. I can't stop his words, their motion heavy, precise, irreversible. He says his cancer is a kind that spreads quickly. The doctors want to start radiation and chemo right away, but they will buy him a year at best. I stare into the fire, numb.

"Lacey."

He strokes the hair at the nape of my neck, coaxing me back, repeating my name as an incantation. The air in the room is neither sour nor sweet, absolutely blank. I study the flames, as if they contain answers. For once in my life, I don't have anything to say.

He speaks in whispers, words like moth wings against my ear. He wants to spend the last months of his life happy. Doesn't want to take any treatment. But he knows that isn't fair to me. The word "fair" flutters through me. His gentle voice could just as easily be explaining to our boys the mysterious path of a boomerang, ways to caulk a window, how to clean grass clippings from a lawnmower blade.

I struggle against him. He hugs and rocks me, hums close to my ear until I quit fighting. Then he sings "Amazing Grace" again, slow and soft. He lifts me, swings me around, wanting to make me laugh. When he plants my feet back down, I ask what in the hell is wrong with him, has he gone crazy?

"I'm dying." He stabs me with the words. "I want to enjoy every last fucking minute."

The excitement in his voice maddens me.

"Lacey, let's do whatever the hell we want."

Want? We? The ache for alcohol rips through me. What I want is sweet bourbon to burn me away.

"One thing I don't want is this." Dewey picks up the Christmas tree and stuffs it in the fireplace, the top heading up the flue. It catches quickly, popping and crackling. He snatches the strings of lights from the floor and flings them into the fire with great relish. I can't move, watching him crash our ornaments against the grate. They shrivel and melt. Paint curls, releasing an odor that reminds me of burnt oil. Strands of tinsel contort and cavort, like snakeheads of Medusa, before going limp. A treetop angel singes and bursts into flames.

For years I've longed to throw the Christmas crap away. Now when Dewey is actually carrying out my desires, I'm not sure they are what I want. Sensing my confusion, he saves a few of the ornaments we bought our first Christmas together, some our grandchildren made. But he tosses everything else into the fire. I lean against the leather, witnessing each transformation.

"Fuck Christmas," Dewey says.

He runs into the dining room, grabs the Christmas cards, and returns to tip them, addressed and stamped, into the fire. He makes a sign of the cross over the fireplace, and says, "Amen."

I ask if he told our sons. No, he isn't sure he will. Wouldn't change anything. No need to railroad their lives. I try not to remember how it took Neville a week to die from his injuries. I don't want to think about watching another person I love die.

Dewey returns to the couch and pulls me against him. He feels tight and strong. Again he describes how the cancer started in his lungs, probably over a year ago, spreading to his spine and ribs, throughout the tissue of his liver. His words, slow and precise, sound as if he's fascinated by the motion and path of his disease. I don't understand.

He plans to quit his job. Wants me to take a leave of absence from the nursing home. Let's sell the house, he says, pare down all our belongings to what fits in a few suitcases, travel to Argentina, learn their version of the tango. One minute his voice sounds level as if describing how to mitre a corner, and then his voice rises to the pitch of someone announcing the birth of a child or the winning of a multi-million lottery.

I begin to reel off all the types of alternative treatments I've heard about: Reiki, Healing Touch, experimental treatments, special studies. I can't name them fast enough.

He whispers my name until I stop talking. "Please let me die the way I want."

His words make it sound so easy. Just let him die the way he wants. But that can't be.

What about what I fucking want? I crash my fist down against the couch arm. I can no longer hold back the tears, which makes me even madder. I hate crying. Unable to hide the anger in my voice, I ask why he didn't go to the doctor if he'd felt bad for that long. He was too caught up in hatred, he says. The final straw was when they released the man who killed our son.

Dewey takes my hand, asks me to promise I'll let go of hatred. I'm not sure I can. Sometimes I think it's the glue that keeps me together, buried so deep it might rip me apart if I ever let it out.

I touch the age spots sprinkled across the backs of his hands. He calls them freckles. I tease that they're meanness coming out.

"What's the count?" he asks.

"You're even now. Seven freckles on each hand." I say that it must be his lucky day, but my voice cracks and the words garble.

"I can just see you in one of those slinky tango dresses." He slides his hands down my sides. "A silk turquoise one that fits close, and then flares at the hem."

I don't snort, as I normally would, or make a snide comment about how horrible my body would look in that kind of revealing dress. He goes on to say we could visit Argentina's Iguazu Falls, Valdes Peninsula to see the herds of seals and sea lions, visit the penguin colony, glacial lakes, an extinct volcano, take a cruise in the Strait of Magellan, go to Tierra del Fuego—the end of the earth. He sounds so sure of himself. I begin to believe it could happen. We have plenty of money saved. Our sons are always encouraging us to travel. They're doing financially well on their own.

We watch the fire in silence. The last embers flail and spark. Have I ever really noticed how many separate colors a blaze contains? The way flames flow like liquid, the way logs split open in chasms, the way livid red blooms from the cracks?

I cannot bear to think of the pain ahead for Dewey. I know only too well, from my work at the nursing home, what cancer can do to a body. But I've also seen the side effects of chemotherapy and radiation treatments. I tell him that maybe while we're in Argentina we can visit some shamans. What I don't tell him, is that maybe if we get away to a foreign country, and really live again, his body might reverse itself, throw off the cancer.

One thing I can say about my husband is he loves to dance. So I'm not surprised when he asks me if I'm up for another dance. I'm not sure my legs will hold me. But in twenty-eight years of marriage, I've never refused a dance with Dewey. Because one thing I know is dancing creates energy, and the movement of two people in harmony generates healing, and my husband has danced me through the worst times of my life. Maybe he'll out-dance the cancer, because Boomer is hard to throw away. He keeps curving back, heading for home.

We rise from the couch. He takes my hand and guides me into a half-turn that spirals me into his arms. We hold each other tight, and I have to tell myself to breathe, just breathe. He presses his lips to my forehead, lingering, before he leans into the first step that will carry us forward.

Acknowledgements

"Constraints," co-winner of Janice Giles Holt Award for Short Fiction, published in *Arts Across Kentucky*

"Cornerstone," Editor's Choice, published in *Still: The Journal*'s Fiction Contest

"Morphing," published in *Louisville Review*

"Palindromes," published in *NonBinary Review*

"Taking Count," published by *Adirondack Review*

"The Floating Child," published in *Stirring*

"To the Man on Crutches Lumbering through Sand Dunes to the Atlantic," published in *Hemingway Shorts Vol. 6* as a contest finalist

"What She Fractured," published in *Inscape*

"Naked," published in *Valparaiso Fiction Review*

I am deeply grateful to the following at Minerva Rising Press for all their work to bring my book into print: Executive Editor Kim Brown, Fiction Editor Nikki Kallio, and Fiction Editorial Assistant Paula Sàbat Martínez. A big thank you to Brooke Schultz for the lovely cover design, and to Judge Anjali Enjeti for selecting my manuscript from the finalists for the Rosemary Daniell Fiction Prize.

about the author

Karen George is the author of five chapbooks and three poetry collections from Dos Madres Press: *Swim Your Way Back* (2014), *A Map and One Year* (2018), and W*here Wind Tastes Like Pears* (2021). Her prose has appeared in *Adirondack Review, Louisville Review, Still: The Journal, Atticus Review, NonBinary Review, Stirring,* and *Hemingway Shorts Vol. 6* as a contest finalist. You can visit her website at: karenlgeorge.blogspot.com.